DEATH ON WIDOW'S WALK

An utterly gripping murder mystery

LESLEY GRANT-ADAMSON

A Rain Morgan Mystery Book 1

Previously published as *Patterns in the Dust*

JOFFE
Ostara
CLASSICS

Revised edition 2023
Joffe Books, London
www.joffebooks.com

First published by Scribner in the USA in 1985 as
Death on Widow's Walk

First published by Faber & Faber in Great Britain
in 1985 as *Patterns in the Dust*

This paperback edition was first published
in Great Britain in 2023

Cover art by Dee Dee Book Covers

ISBN: 978-1-83526-300-6

For Andrew who took me to Somerset

CHAPTER 1

October was dying. Brown hills, brambled lanes. A softly focused sea curving across a wide bay. Black and white cows ambled into the road, invited by a shirt-sleeved farmer. Rain Morgan slowed her car to match their pace, then gently pulled on the handbrake and gave time to the view.

'Hurry's only a habit,' she said aloud. 'A bad habit.' She smiled.

She cut the engine, reached for a boiled sweet and got out of the car. She leaned against its red bonnet, then opted for the nearby gate, her elbows bare on warm wood, her blonde curls stroked by a warm westerly breeze.

Her smile refused to go away. 'It's like . . .' she began to tell herself and cast around for comparison. The last day of school when the future yawned freedom? The start of the per-fect holiday? Or a new love affair? But no, it wasn't like any of those. It was a perfect moment, a rare time when mood and circumstance were in tune. There were no 'if onlys', there were no 'buts'.

She was even pleased to be pleased to be alone. Oliver ought to have come, meant to until a colleague's baby arrived early and upset plans. 'So what?' Rain said when Oliver told her. 'If the paper is handing out paternity leave then it's their

1

problem. They'll have to get a freelance to cover. Why expect you to give up your break?'

But Oliver wasn't willing to risk another cartoonist winning over his audience and so he had stayed in London. Early that morning, Rain crept out of their flat and drove west. She would miss Oliver. In a day or two, of course she would. They had been in each other's lives a long time. Three years. For each of them that was a long time.

Soon after he had come from Australia to London she had met him, been attracted by his effervescent humour. Most cartoonists she knew were sombre worriers. She watched him ease his way into a job on the *Post*, uncertain how far she was being used, whether it mattered. Oliver could be ruthless, too.

When they had rows — and they often had rows — she reminded him that if it hadn't been for her he'd still be in a bedsitter in Earls Court. Unfair. Untrue. But the ammunition that came to hand during rows often was.

By now the cows were a blur entering the yard of a faded pink farmhouse. One last look at wheatears practising loops and whirls for the flight from winter, another sweep of the hump of hills and the sheen of the bay, and Rain was ready to move on. The village lay barely a mile ahead.

Opening the car door she noticed that morning's *Post* lying on the back seat, her byline picture gazing up from the gossip column. She turned the paper over. Perhaps she ought to change her name while she was staying here? 'Rain' had grown from a childish misspelling to become a usefully distinctive byline, but it could not offer anonymity. She toyed with a name or two. It might be nice to be a Barbara or a Judy for a few weeks.

Yet she was sure to be recognized and besides, Adam Hollings, whose cottage she was borrowing, might have heralded her arrival. She did not know Adam Hollings. He was Oliver's cousin, who had followed him from Australia, and so Oliver had made the arrangements. The arrangements, she feared, were a little loose.

Oliver spent much time telling her how she would love Nether Hampton and how charming Withy Cottage was. But he confessed the night before she set off that he had not spoken to Adam.

'But it'll be all right,' he said airily, 'Adam said we could use the place any time he isn't there and he's always away in the autumn.'

They stood there in the bedroom, Rain's half-packed rollbag on the bed between them, and argued it out. She felt it was all too vague. He insisted Adam would never had given him a key and told him to 'come any time' if he hadn't meant it. She made Oliver phone Withy Cottage again. And again. But there was no reply, as there had been no reply all along.

'There you are,' Oliver said. She gave in, finished filling the rollbag. He went back to the television.

The plain grey stone tower of Nether Hampton church grew closer and the lane swung into a cobbled market square. A hunt was meeting there. Hounds lolloped over children who'd come to pat. Horses scented excitement. Onlookers milled across the square or lounged against colour-washed houses bordering it.

Rain tucked her car into the roadside and got out. A dappled grey with a nervous manner and an elderly moustached rider backed into it, and were cross to find it there. Rain refused to catch the rider's querulous eye, and his spluttering disgust was wasted.

'Hope you're not in a hurry,' a man's voice said beside her. 'They'll be moving off soon but there's no chance of getting through until they do.' Thirtyish, her sort of age. Casually dressed, not tweedy, not one of the hunting set. Later she would remember the things he was not. Not tall. Not striking in appearance. Not a risk taker. Not like Oliver.

She smiled back. 'I'm at journey's end. Or will be once I've found Withy Cottage.'

'Withy Cottage?' Surprise, not just repetition. 'You know it?'

He pointed across the square. 'The blue one. You've found it.'

Just the right shade of blue, not too frivolous and not too sombre. She had grown up with her aunt's tenet that blue was a tricky colour, that the wrong shade could look cheap. Withy Cottage looked good with its well-chosen blue and its white woodwork. And it was pleasing in its proportions although, as Oliver had promised, quite tiny.

She was remarking that it was charming (Oliver's description, too) when the dappled grey got into more trouble. Everyone's attention was drawn by the angry exchange between its rider and a tall impressive man leading his mount. The incident was over in seconds but it had its effect on the crowd. A happy mood was broken. Shortly after, the riders prepared to move off.

'The moustached man on the grey is the General, he'll be your next-door neighbour,' the man beside Rain told her.

'Who was he fighting with?'

'Sir James Alcombe, lord of the manor. You'll find Nether Hampton has all the correct ingredients: local gentry, wealthy incomers who've retired here, and the ragtag and bobtail who keep the place alive.'

Rain encouraged him and discovered that the middle-aged woman with the carefully coiffured hair, the purple tweed suit and the quivering chihuahua in her arms lived in the house behind the high wall and elaborate iron gates; that the General's wife was the elegant woman with the superior air; that the dumpy rosy-cheeked rector was too High for the tastes of the village but in recompense had written a lively local history; and that the green-haired lad with the baby face contorted into a scowl had gone all the way to Taunton to buy his green hair.

'And Adam Hollings? Do you know where he's gone?' He didn't. Only that Adam was always 'flitting off' but this time no one knew where.

He shrugged. 'You know what Adam's like.' The square was emptying as the last of the horses trotted by, sun bouncing off their sleekness and polished harnesses. It was a well-turned-out hunt, the standard set by Sir James Alcombe and aspired to by the rest. Only the General, still tussling with the dappled grey, failed miserably in manner and appearance to come up to muster.

Traffic was inching on its way. Rain turned to her car, eager to fetch the cottage key and let herself in. 'All you haven't told me,' she said, 'is who you are. I'm Rain Morgan, holiday-maker.' She held out her hand in mock formality.

'Robin Woodley, archaeologist. Digging up Nether Hampton castle.' With equal gravity he shook her hand.

'You didn't tell me there was a castle!'

He gestured vaguely across the square. 'Over there. Beyond the church.' He was backing away, leaving as everyone else was leaving. 'See you up there sometime?' He raised a hand in farewell and was gone.

Rain took her leather shoulder bag and the cottage key from the car and walked over to Withy Cottage. She would work out later where best to park. The pretty blue and white house was set in a higgledy-piggledy row of buildings that counted for much of the village. Its stiff door yielded to a determined shove. Then she was standing in an untidy living room. Long, narrow and with a large open fireplace where logs waited for a match.

The open door gave light as she unfastened shutters and folded them back into recesses. The cottage was stuffy. Soot had fallen on to the logs and tainted the air. Rain opened the living-room window and went to explore the rest.

Beyond the living room with its country furniture was a square kitchen with a slate worktop, pine cupboards and a brown floorcovering. The window opened on to the garden but the ground-floor extension cut the garden view to a few yards, and showed instead a boundary fence and, further, a gentle hill.

From the kitchen, a door led to a short lobby. There were two other doors off this: one to the garden, the other to a compact modern bathroom which had once been a coal

5

or wood shed. Above the living room and kitchen were two bedrooms.

Throughout, the cottage had been modernized, decorated and furnished simply, enhancing its old world atmosphere without descending to nostalgic nonsense. She approved of Adam Hollings's taste, and she began the game of piecing together his personality from his things. He was a gadget man, no doubt of that. Withy Cottage had sacrificed none of its rural 300-year-old charm to his need for comfort, but it now contained many of the toys of the modern age.

A television set perched among the bookshelves, a video recorder sat on the shelf beneath it, its digital clock blinking the time. A portable computer was tucked neatly under a worn pine desk. On the desk was an electronic typewriter and on a nearby shelf the grey plastic interface which could link the typewriter to the computer so that it worked as a printer.

Beside the interface was another grey plastic shape, a telephone answering machine. With it was a slim black box, the remote-control device for listening to callers' messages by dialling the Withy Cottage number from any other phone. Adam Hollings had left the machine switched off.

The kitchen had benefited, too, from Adam Hollings's interest in equipment. Coffee was made in an electric filter machine, and his powerful food processor would have a hundred uses for anyone at all imaginative about cooking. Rain believed he was: a short selection of good, well-thumbed cookery books stood on a shelf. On a wall rack nearby a graded series of top-quality Sabatier knives had a used and businesslike appearance. The enamelled cast-iron pot and the heavy earthenware casserole dish were chosen not merely for good looks but because they did the job superbly. She found nothing in Withy Cottage which had not earned its place on both counts.

Her final impression, like her first, was that the house was clean but the living room dishevelled. Books leaned awkwardly on shelves, papers spilled from a wire rack on the desk. Automatically she tidied and straightened. Then she went the few steps to the village shop to buy ground coffee and milk.

The kitchen cupboard where she found china was orderly enough. She switched on the filter machine and while it gurgled to itself she fetched the car and parked it conveniently outside the cottage door. Nether Hampton had not succumbed to parking restrictions.

Once the coffee was poured Rain chose a basket chair in the living room and curled up there with her mug. One or two passing faces peeped curiously in at her but otherwise all was peace. The *Post* and its problems could be a million miles away. Oliver was right. This was just the place to forget them. Better still to consider them coolly.

The paper was going through one of its periodic glooms, seeking out scapegoats to carry the blame for its failure to fight off a rival's circulation challenge. Culpability had nothing to do with it. She had seen it happen before. A few faces would change, for a while the gods would be appeased and then it would begin all over again.

The problems, as Oliver insisted, brushing them aside, were not hers. She could do nothing about them, she ought to ignore them. But she found it hard to watch a colleague ill-treated, tension created deliberately to persuade him to leave. In the end he would have to go because someone else had been promised his job. Once the offer was made, at a dinner party, it was only a matter of when the new man came.

'It's an everyday story of journalists,' Oliver said. 'You know that and I know that. If Tom is out and Jerry is in, then the sooner Tom actually gets out the happier for everyone.'

She retorted that Tom had nowhere to go and there was no excuse for persecuting him. Oliver argued that was emotional, and that the only course for the rest of them was to ignore what was going on.

She wondered aloud how Oliver would feel if he were ever to find himself in Tom's position. But it was not a point for discussion. Oliver could not imagine himself as anybody's victim.

'You always see things from the underdog's point of view,' he said, exasperated, as though this were a base error. 'The *Post* has a point, too: he hasn't been contributing much lately.'

'Isn't that the way it works? Apply the pressure until he can't cope and then they *do* have an excuse to get rid of him? Tom's your friend and you're keeping away from him at a time when he needs friends . . .'

He snorted. 'I'm not getting involved. If there was something I could do . . . If there was something anyone could do . . .'

She waited but the sentence hung incomplete. They lapsed into silence, Oliver flicking through the television guide, Rain thinking unflattering thoughts about him.

Her long holiday, accumulated and then delayed because of an especially busy period at the *Post*, came at the right time for her to escape the gathering storm. Quite possibly the victim would accept defeat and retreat before she went back.

Among the books on Adam Hollings's shelves Rain noticed a slim history of the village. She hooked it out. A modest foreword, in which the Reverend Clifford Hadley thanked everyone who had rendered him any kind of assistance, confirmed that it was the book Robin Woodley had mentioned. She began to read.

The index led her to a section on the castle: a Norman ruin but with substantial chunks standing. There were several pages on its violent past, some fact, some fiction. It began with William the Conqueror, continued with robber barons, fell into the hands of heretics, and passed, a few generations ago, into the possession of Sir James Alcombe's family. An early source wrote that 'ye mote did runne with blood' after an unsuccessful siege. Another writer was more interested in defenestration and hauntings. The rector, too, relished his bit of shock and horror, quoting in considerable and unnecessary detail some of the more unpleasant goings on.

The church clock reminded Rain that she had yet to buy food for lunch. She dropped the book on the desk on her way to the kitchen sink with her empty mug. Through the window, movement caught her eye. The hunt flew across the hill, bright in autumn sun. Darting ahead of it, ran the fox. She hoped very much for his miraculous escape.

It was while Rain was watching the hunt that Robin Woodley was discovering the first body.

CHAPTER 2

Withy Cottage had an iron knocker and its sudden clamour startled Rain who was about to go to the shop. She turned to the door but the handle was already moving. Robin Woodley burst in.

'Please, I must use your phone.' He brushed past her in the narrow room and headed for Adam's desk. He was pale, tense. Quite unlike the relaxed figure who had dropped into conversation with her an hour ago.

'Whatever's happened?' The front door gaped. She ignored it, followed him down the room. 'What is it?'

A voice from the telephone was speaking to him: 'Emergency, which service do you require?' And he was asking for the police.

'There's a body . . .' he began, but first the professionally calm voice wanted to know who he was and where he was calling from. Then it let him say he had found a body in Nether Hampton castle.

When it was over, when he had been asked to meet the police at the castle in as long as it took to get the nearest patrol car there, he replaced the receiver and just stood. Rain said briskly: 'Why don't you sit down?' She gestured firmly to the sofa.

Then she whisked open the dresser cupboard, found what she hoped for. 'I don't know Adam but I'm sure he wouldn't mind under the circumstances.' She splashed whisky into a glass and took it to him. 'Now,' she said, 'tell me about it. You found a body?'

He nodded, cradled the glass in his hands. 'I dug it up. Not where I am really working, this was on the other side of the castle. I'm not meant to be there.' A pause, a sip. 'Yesterday I decided to take a look anyway, I thought there was a well. I went back up there this morning to poke around a bit more. And there it was, in the well.'

He shuddered, looked as though he was about to explain further but instead dashed to the bathroom. A black labrador stuck its nose into Withy Cottage reminding Rain to close the door. The cistern flushed distantly.

Afterwards Rain went with Robin Woodley to the castle. His colour was returning and the shock of the unpleasant discovery was over. They had to walk through the churchyard to join the path to the castle. Several other paths branched off it and he managed the joke that all paths led to the graveyard.

He apologized for bursting in on her. 'I'm staying at the pub, but there's only a payphone in the passage and if I'd used that the whole village would have been up there and staring by now.'

'And the public callbox is out of order.'

'Yes, how did you know?'

'I believe they always are.'

He gave a short laugh. 'As long as Nether Hampton has got Wayne Chidgey this one always will be. He's the green-haired lad.'

'The village vandal?' They were approaching the castle now, the route taking them around ancient earthworks. Norman walls peeped through a veil of fading autumn foliage.

'That's our Wayne. I caught him hanging around my car in the pub car park one evening, not that there was anything worth stealing — least of all the car — and he can't drive. He just makes one nervous.' Another path crossed the one they

11

were following and Rain hesitated. 'This way,' Robin said and went ahead. It was now too narrow for them to walk side by side and so they grew silent.

Rain could not see the castle although she knew they were very close to it. Unkempt trees met above her head, crowded so thickly on each side of the track she had the impression she was in a fair-sized wood. Even in leafless winter the castle would be a secret place.

Robin stopped and turned back to her. 'Careful over the bridge. It's lost a few planks.'

They had arrived. Peering passed him she saw the dilapidated access to the ruin. The path flowed smoothly up to a wooden bridge over the moat which had once 'runne with blood'. Centuries had filled much of its depth and trees grew there now. What remained of the gatehouse and flanking walls appeared sturdy, although ivy trickled over them and shrubs had rooted on top.

Robin ignored faded red Keep Out signs threatening Danger and led the way in. 'What do you think?' he said. Rain made appropriate murmurs. She had no idea how one judged such a thing.

Beyond the gatehouse was the enclosed near-circle of the castle, an area largely overgrown with scruffy shrubs and saplings. She could make out now the remnant of the walls — grey stone achieving perhaps twenty feet in places and interrupted with the remains of towers. There were long gaps where the wall had vanished, presumably tumbled into the moat.

She followed Robin into the enclosure where he stopped again. 'It's over there,' he said, gesturing as vaguely as he had done that morning when he'd told her of the existence of the castle. 'The body, I mean.'

He didn't want to go near it again. Rain, hoping aloud, said she expected the police would arrive at any moment. She was hungry. The sooner the police came the better, then she would leave.

Meanwhile Robin showed her the site where he had been working. They were outside the wall now, looking at a patch of cleared ground where soil had been carefully removed to reveal the different shades of the layers of earth.

'There should have been a thorough dig years ago. It's unlikely to be an important site but it's interesting because so much of the twelfth-century building remains, and its history is well documented too,' he said.

Rain joked that it was all so overgrown it looked as though no one had been near it since the twelfth century.

'It is private land and the owner — Sir James Alcombe — hardly encourages visitors. He's responsible for the Keep Out signs, and insists the place is dangerous. But you'd be surprised how many people do come. Quite a few of the locals pop in to see what I'm up to.'

He said that Mrs Murray, the widow with the purple suit and the chihuahua, walked that way morning and evening with her dog; that Wayne Chidgey, the village villain, lurked and, given half a chance, tampered; that the rector was always trotting up with words of encouragement, because it was mainly through his pressure that Sir James had agreed to an excavation.

'And Adam Hollings,' he concluded, 'says that in the evenings it's the local trysting place.'

She was glad he'd mentioned Adam. It gave her the chance to piece together some more information about her absent host. She needed to know how soon he was likely to be home and wanting Withy Cottage to himself.

But before the question was out the police came, tramping heavily along the path, clumping over the broken boards of the bridge. There were two of them, a stocky sergeant of indeterminate age and a spindly young constable. They came through the gatehouse looking up and about them like dogs sniffing the informative air.

Rain did not intend to see the body. Robin Woodley glumly led the two policemen to where it lay and Rain, having explained her presence, felt free to leave. She took a final look at the curl of the castle wall and made her way to the gatehouse.

The sergeant's deep rumbling voice and Robin's responses came clearly across to her, bounced from the grey walls. Then there was the crackle of a radio.

This, she thought, could well be her only visit to the castle. The police would keep everyone away while they searched, and because of the overgrown state of the site that could be a lengthy process. She crossed the bridge and set off down the path.

At the point where another one crossed it she came upon a lean, tweed-suited man, hesitating. He had set down a large bag and was considering the merits of three possible directions.

Rain called over: 'The castle's up this way.'

'Thanks.' He stooped for the bag.

'I'll show you.'

'Thanks again.'

'You're the pathologist?'

'Edward Markell. I see my bag gives me away.' A brief smile and he fell into step behind her.

She led him to the castle and to the body. He said: 'Good afternoon, Sergeant Willett, PC Smith,' and dropped on his knees to look closely at the reason for his Saturday afternoon being disrupted.

Only a small part of the body was exposed, Robin Woodley having fled once he realized quite what he was unearthing. Dr Markell disturbed nothing. He pulled a notebook from a pocket, grunted, shifted his position, wrote.

'Been there some time, sir,' said the sergeant, matter-of-factly. PC Smith blew his thin nose.

Dr Markell stood up, brushed dry earth from the knees of his tweed trousers. He looked around. 'Time your chaps were here with their cameras, isn't it, Ted?'

Sergeant Willett pursed his plump lips. 'Don't think they were expecting this, sir. The message was an archaeologist had unearthed a body. Made it sound like Roman remains, not a bloody murder.'

'I see.'

They all looked down where the body, not much more than a skeleton, jutted from the soil. Sergeant Willett said: 'How long do you think . . . ?'

'I'll answer that once it's fully uncovered and I can see what we've got,' said Dr Markell. 'But it's not in what's usually termed 'a shallow grave', is it?'

'The archaeologist says it's an old well, sir.' As he spoke, Willett glanced towards Robin who was standing with Rain a little way off.

'And the conditions in an old well could have slowed the rate of decomposition. Dampness and the type of material filling the well will have had an effect, so I'll be taking some of this back to the lab.' His toecap prodded the neat pile of earth Robin Woodley had set aside as he dug down. A little scree ran down the mound and fell silently on to the skull. PC Smith blew his nose again.

Detectives came then, more short square men puffing their way up the path. More uniformed men followed. Rain left.

When she emerged from the path into the churchyard she was amused to see a sizeable group of villagers gathered around the police vehicles and Dr Markell's car. Wayne Chidgey was among them.

'Something going on up at the castle?' an overweight middle-aged jolly man asked her.

Rain said Yes — a body had been found. The crowd savoured its ripple of horror.

The green head bobbed towards the churchyard gate. 'You don't want to go nosing up there,' a broad-faced woman called sharply to the lad. 'D'ye hear, Wayne? You come back here, now.'

But Wayne was through the iron gate and weaving between the tombstones. 'Ee don't never do a thing you say, Doris,' the jolly man commiserated.

Rain was less lucky in her escape. The crowd was a hoop around her, pressing for information. Where was it? Who was it? Who found it? Oh, that would upset that nice Mr Woodley, that would.

They would not let her free until they were satisfied that she could not or would not tell them more. They were pleasant and friendly, and quite compelling. Short of backing into the

15

churchyard and making off the way she had come there was no escape from them. It was both funny and a little unnerving.

At last they relented and she went directly to the village shop. Good, there was no one in there apart from Mrs Wall, the middle-aged owner in the flowered overall. They had met earlier when Rain bought the coffee and milk and had already exchanged pleasantries about Rain's holiday in Nether Hampton.

No one had left the crowd at the church gate yet so she would not be held up repeating her story. They knew very well that Rain was only the small fry. There were the police, the pathologist and the body to come through the churchyard yet. They weren't going to miss any of that.

Rain filled a wire basket and took it to the till. Mrs Wall smiled a little shyly at her. 'You're Rain Morgan, aren't you? In the *Post*.'

Rain smiled back. 'So I am.' Her photograph watched from the paper Mrs Wall had been reading to while away the time between customers.

The till began to sing, the purchases swung from the basket to a carrier bag, Rain got her money ready to pay and be gone. Then Mrs Wall said: 'Terrible, isn't it? About that body up at the castle. Did Robin Woodley find it?'

Rain maintained her smile. Yes, it was terrible. Yes, he had. She walked back to Withy Cottage wondering however did they do it? Information seemed to be disseminated in the air, like pollen. A few facts were handed over at the church gate and moments later there they were in the village shop apparently by magic.

She made herself a meal which was neither lunch nor tea but would do for both. The air had cooled and she wondered whether to light the logs that evening or whether there was an electric fire she could plug in instead. She hadn't noticed one but it could be in a cupboard.

After eating and washing up she began the hunt. There was no light in the cupboard under the stairs and no torch so she gave that up as hopeless and looked in the other rooms.

The stairs themselves did not steal space from the long thin living room but hid behind a door leading off it. They wound up beside the deep chimney. In the bedroom above the living room there was a high wall cupboard, also making use of the space beside the chimney. It was locked.

A mahogany wardrobe, so large that it must have been assembled in the room, stood against the end wall looking over at a small window. There was a fitted carpet and twin beds. The only other furniture was a rough deal table, beech chairs and a table adequate for a small desk or a dressing table as need arose. The wardrobe was empty except for a few wire hangers which chattered after she closed the door on them. The table drawer yielded no cupboard key.

The other bedroom was square with a catslide roof sloping down to a low window with a sill deep enough for a window seat. Sitting there, above the kitchen, Rain could see along the roof of the back lobby and bathroom and down the garden. The end wall was made up of a row of uncared-for stone sheds. Beyond was some open land and then a cottage facing away from Withy Cottage. The view ended with the rise crowned with a wood. If it had not been for that hill, Withy Cottage would have seen the bay.

This room also had two single beds, a polished ancient pine chest with its bun feet missing, and a metal trunk containing spare blankets. The pine chest was empty.

Thoughtfully, Rain closed both bedroom doors, went downstairs and through the kitchen to the back lobby. This was empty except for a basket of logs and a thick rubber-backed doormat pushed up against the ill-fitting back door which fastened with a heavy bolt. The only cupboard here housed nothing but an immersion heater.

The bathroom had the usual fittings and a mirror-fronted wall cupboard. A frosted-glass window was set in the same run of wall as the back door.

Returning to the kitchen Rain systematically went through all the cupboards and drawers. She found neatly stacked saucepans and crockery, a full range of good-quality utensils arranged in compartmented drawers, a neat arrangement for storing dusters and cleaning materials. And, with spare light bulbs, she found a torch.

Now she had the torch she probed the stair cupboard and backed out triumphant with an electric fire. Then she delved further in and emerged dragging a suitcase. It opened and revealed a matching, smaller one. In that was a third. In that was a squashy travel bag and inside that some rollbags of various sizes. It was like a less pretty version of a nest of Russian dolls.

Rain perched on the edge of the basket chair and considered the haul spread over the blue carpet. Then she methodically put everything except the electric fire back exactly as she had found it.

Withy Cottage was easily the neatest house she had ever stayed in. Yet she had arrived to find the living room untidy. She was getting her first suspicion that something was wrong.

She settled back in the basket chair and thought about it. She was still there when Dr Markell's car whisked over the cobbled square. The pathologist was leaving, but the police would be in Nether Hampton much longer.

CHAPTER 3

Early in the evening, Rain telephoned Oliver and after the preliminaries about the ease of her journey and the trivial round of his day she told him about the body in the castle.

'You promised me a quiet sleepy little place,' she said. 'This village is alive with policemen.'

'There's nothing like a good murder on the doorstep to take your mind off other matters,' said Oliver brightly, reminding her of what she had managed to forget.

She let it pass. 'Look, about Adam . . .'

'Oh no, not again. You're there, he's not — so what's the problem?'

'Only that nobody here knows when he went or where he went or when he's due back . . .'

'He doesn't have to report his movements. Knowing Adam, he likes to keep people guessing.'

'But Oliver, this living room was in a mess . . .'

He was laughing, deliberately misunderstanding. 'Oh I see, you want to have it out with him that you've borrowed his home, maybe not entirely with his permission, and he wasn't good enough to clean it up for you!'

She gave up and changed the subject, although it did not escape her notice that Oliver was now conceding that perhaps she ought not to be there. 'How soon can you come? Even if it's only for a weekend?' He didn't know and didn't know when he might know. She did not press although she felt he might have tried harder.

Oliver had a message for her from Holly Chase, her deputy on the *Post* gossip column, passing on a bit of news that would interest Rain greatly but would not make the paper. The lawyers would have seen to it that it didn't.

Holly was lively, leggy and had a disarming telephone manner that made her superb at her job. People who met her first when her beautiful voice soothed them down a telephone line were not prepared for Holly in person. Holly Chase was black. She played it up with skinny little plaits that jangled with beads, and she wore fashionably outrageous clothes. Holly Chase was not to be ignored.

'Holly says you're to enjoy yourself and stay as long as you like, she's not going to pinch your job,' Oliver reported.

'Would you believe a journalist who told you that? It's incitement to drive straight back to the office.'

After a few more minutes there was a diminuendo of goodbyes, the promise to telephone again, and they rang off. Whatever he said, she knew that Oliver would not come to Nether Hampton until he was quite ready to. Holly had, with admirable perception, been doubtful about Rain's tactic of setting off on the assumption that Oliver would follow in decent haste. Rain had known it too, but had reached the stage where a holiday alone was better than no holiday at all. While Oliver's energy would carry him through the year without a pause if he wasn't coerced into one, she felt the need.

'But you're to post him on to me first class,' she'd told Holly, enlisting her help.

Holly had nodded solemnly, the beaded plaits clinking prettily. 'Male order,' she said.

When she'd heard Oliver put the phone down, Rain stood and listened to the silence of Withy Cottage. She did not care for silence. It was one of the country things that always came freshly surprising. In London the buzz of the city was there night and day, one was demonstrably never alone. Nether Hampton without Oliver, without the sounds of other people's activity, threatened loneliness.

Obligingly the fridge started up its warm companionable noise. Rain smiled at it, caught herself doing so, smiled at herself. It was quite easy to understand how people living alone developed the habit of talking to themselves.

The fridge made her think about food. It ought to be time to eat something but her mealtimes were out of kilter and she wasn't hungry yet. Instead, she bathed, changed from jeans, blouse and sweater into a vivid knitted dress, coloured tights and low blue shoes. Then she sat and read another chunk of the rector's history of the village.

When she judged she'd waited long enough, she set the book aside and picked up her shoulder bag. The day had been rather full of Robin Woodley already but she had to see him again.

The pub across the square was called the Huntsman, and was what visitors to the West Country hoped to see. The roof was thatched, not too recently. There were flower tubs by the porch with autumn displays of chrysanthemums.

Inside were two stone-flagged bars. In the smarter one a once gaudy carpet had worn to drabness. The Huntsman had encouragingly few beams, meaning they were genuine. Capacious hearths held smouldering logs on deep beds of ash.

The carpeted bar was almost empty, the other half full. Several friendly faces smiled or said a word of greeting to Rain. A number she recognized from the hunt meet that morning, others from the church gate. Some she was sure she had not seen before. She had hoped that Robin Woodley would be there, so that she need not ask for him.

At the bar she disturbed a large ginger cat nestled beside the beer pumps. The landlady, Betty Yeo, hurrying through from the other bar, appeared unaware of the cat. Rain shied away from the Huntsman's white wine, asked first for a gin and tonic and then for Robin Woodley.

21

Betty Yeo, a dowdy bustling woman teasing the seams of a tight frock, rang up the money and handed over the change before replying that she'd see if he was in. 'Who'll I say?' she said, looking over her shoulder, already on her way out of the bar. She had a loud voice.

'Rain Morgan.'

'Who?'

Again. Louder.

A lot of nudging was going on. 'There you are,' said the jolly man who had been at the church gate. 'I said it was her.' He turned to Rain. 'I told 'em it were.'

Rain smiled back over her glass. There was a bit of banter, no single remark distinguishable. A very old man leaned closer and shouted into her ear. 'Now what I've always wanted to know about them gossip columns . . .'

Robin appeared. The old man never asked his question, as the rest of them enjoyed some noisy fun at Robin's expense. There were tables and chairs in the room but only Rain and Robin left the huddle at the bar. They could talk in reasonable privacy.

'It's Adam Hollings,' Rain said soon, getting to the point. 'I was going to ask you this morning. Or afternoon, or whenever it all was. The day got a bit complicated.'

'What about Adam?' He sounded just a shade guarded.

She told him. There was a lengthy pause, during which Rain heard a voice at the bar begin a story about a carnival float. Then he said: 'I've told you what I know about Adam. He goes away quite often; this time he didn't mention he was going to.'

Rain sipped her drink, then said: 'Do you mind if we start at the beginning of this?' And without waiting for a response plunged on. 'You must be a friend of Adam Hollings. I don't even know him. He's the cousin of a friend.' How else, she wondered, to describe her undulating relationship with Oliver?

Robin said: 'I don't remember saying I was a friend.'

'No, but you knew exactly where his telephone is. You knew where to find his bathroom. You are familiar with the cottage so you knew him well enough to visit him.'

He admitted it. 'OK, I knew him well enough for that.'

'Now. Was it usual for the shutters in the living room to be closed when he was away?'

He shrugged. 'I haven't noticed.' She waited while he thought about it, watching the firelight dance on his beer.

Then: 'I've been here three months. He's been away once before in that time. Briefly. But I think . . . no, I'm sure the shutters were open then. I remember now. I came out of here one evening and Wayne Chidgey and some of his pals were hanging around near Withy Cottage. One of them was peering in. I went over when they'd left just to make certain they hadn't done any damage. They hadn't.'

It didn't mean a thing, Rain knew that. The time the shutters were left open could just as easily have been the odd time out. Then Robin said: 'If you're bothered about the shutters then you ought to be talking to Doris Chidgey, not me. She cleans the cottage for Adam so she'd know what the routine is.'

'I'll do that.'

From the Huntsman they drove in Rain's car to Yethercombe, a village high on the Quantocks and overlooking the bay. Neither of them had eaten and Robin promised the pub there did good bar food. There was a restaurant too, for more formal dining, and Saturday night couples celebrating birthdays and other special occasions made their way to it. But the bar meals were served in comfort and warmth and Rain was relaxed and happy.

Robin Woodley was good undemanding company, questioning about the *Daily Post* and the gossip business without making her spend more than a fraction of her evening on it. In turn, she was gentle with his work and life, successfully resisting the impulse that made journalists unremitting interviewers. She learned that in a very few weeks he was to join a team on a major excavation in the Middle East and was filling in time carrying out the Nether Hampton work for an archaeological trust. The work had been delayed and hampered and generally unsatisfactory. But now it was nearly over and while the rest of Nether Hampton was facing up to the cold damp days ahead, he was cheered by the promised change of scene.

This was not his first acquaintance with Nether Hampton. He had spent part of his youth at the harbour town of Portlet, not many miles along the coast, and knew the county well. On the way downhill to the village, Rain pulled in at a view-point, where he showed her the distant seaside resorts on the English and Welsh sides of the Bristol Channel, identifying them by their straggles of lights in the darkness.

He left her outside Withy Cottage, quickly, saving her from having to ask him in. His footsteps rang over the cobbles. As she hung her knitted dress in the wardrobe she saw a light appear under the Huntsman's thatch and then curtains masked it.

Rain slept in the smaller of the bedrooms, the square back room with its sloping ceiling and country view. She found a hook for her dressing gown and she made up the bed with sheets and pillow case which had come in her rollbag. Her spare pair, for when Oliver came, were slipped into a drawer of the pine chest. Adam Hollings, she thought, as she tucked in the final corner, would have been better organized than this. He would have done his bedmaking before sinking into a chair with a book or going out for the evening.

She felt she now knew a lot about Adam Hollings. Piecing together what Oliver and Robin had told her, adding her own observation, she knew that he had given up steady work (something to do with computers) several years ago when he had come into some money. He had inherited from an aunt in Australia who had written a book called *Publicans and Sinners*, which showed no signs of ever going out of print.

Adam had announced he was dropping out of the rat race (London), drifted around the globe for a time and then discovered Nether Hampton (no one knew how), bought Withy Cottage and more or less settled down. He needed to earn only a modest amount and managed that in a haphazard way. He was supposed to be a writer but no one had seen anything he had written. Rain smiled as she remembered Oliver admitting to it. They'd agreed they both knew journalists like that, and at least two were currently on the *Post*.

One of Adam's working trips always took place in the autumn. Neither Oliver nor Robin knew how long it usually lasted, but Robin thought Adam had already been gone a month — and then amended that to at least a month.

Rain yawned and got into bed. She'd ask Doris Chidgey all about it.

She took up the rector's history again. It taught her about the castle and the church, about Laurel House across the square where Mrs Murray and her chihuahua lived, and about Sir James Alcombe's home, Nether Hampton Hall. It showed her the way national events had touched this remote place from Saxon through to modern times.

A Saxon king had held court nearby; the Normans and their barons had made it of regional importance; Roundheads and Cavaliers had fought over it; in the village square men had been hanged, drawn and quartered for their part in the Monmouth Uprising; and a village lad had become a founder of the Trades Union movement.

Nether Hampton was a typical sleepy little English village which history had never allowed a minute's peace. Beyond the famous events, and tucked away behind the rector's enthusiastic prose about castle, church and landed gentry, was the common thread of the villagers. The chroniclers from Domesday to the rector had no room for the preoccupations of the people whose lives were the place — the pettinesses, the joys, the inviolable pecking order.

From its history came the legends the village half-believed. The rector treated them kindly. Dimly remembered Celtic saints crossed the sea from Ireland and Wales in unlikely craft and did unlikelier things before sailing back. Ghost stories had their genesis in fallen men coming home from the Battle of Sedgemoor.

The puzzle of the ammonite-rich shore was explained by St Keyna's success in turning snakes to stone. Curving snail-like fossils were 'devil's toenails'.

The castle was thought to be haunted, not by the victims of the siege when 'ye mote did runne with blood' but, more romantically, by the heartbroken widow of a baron. He had been killed in battle. Her family negotiated to remarry her to another warlord, a liaison which from their point of view had many merits and from hers none.

Before the wedding she flung herself from a tower and died. Her ghost was supposed to have been seen frequently (the rector was very careful with his 'supposes') fleeing along the path from the castle to the church. 'No map has ever given that mean track a name,' wrote the Reverend Clifford Hadley, 'but Nether Hampton has always known it as the Widow's Walk.' He had come to the end of his chapter, a good place to close the book and sleep. Rain did.

She was soon awake again, staring into impenetrable country darkness, listening to the deepest of silences broken eventually by the reassuring hum of the fridge in the kitchen below. The emptiness of the world outside made her uncomfortable. She was used to skies that never grew black, to the constant sounds of a busy world close by.

Oliver said it was inexplicable, a fear of the dark. What did she imagine was there which wasn't present in daylight? Who did she think would be waiting to pounce? There were no answers for him. She had none to offer and Oliver, scared of no one and nothing, could not picture the uneasy chill that seeped through her when she was alone somewhere strange and the light had gone.

To defuse the fear she had thought it through and through, on sunlit afternoons when it was as foolish to her as to anyone else.

The best explanation she could offer was the story of her nanny, Clara, who was locked accidentally in a cellar at Rain's aunt's Victorian house. Clara was there almost an hour before the family, coming in from the garden, heard her distress and freed her.

Rain remembered being held aloft in her aunt's arms and watching Clara emerge, sobbing and frightened. Then

Rain had given way to equal misery. For weeks afterwards Rain suffered nightmares and tearful bedtimes, then her aunt brought her nightlights.

Perhaps Clara's terror had created Rain's fear. Perhaps Rain had caught it, like chicken pox, from her. Or perhaps Rain had been born with it deep within her and Clara's experience was the catalyst which released it.

Only someone as close to her as Oliver would guess at her fear. When Holly Chase envied her the ability to handle anyone and any situation, it was nearly true. Rain had made it so, compensating, maybe, for the irrational childhood fear she could not put aside.

Soon, she knew, the fridge would cease its tune and the silence would be as perfect as the darkness. Before that happened she drew the blankets over her head and waited for sleep, occupying her mind with the day's extraordinary events.

When she did sleep she was caught up in a dream in which Adam Hollings was the quarry as police rode with hounds through Nether Hampton. And then Tom, who was being ousted from the *Post*, was to be hanged for being on the losing side. Rain was acutely aware that everyone had got everything wrong, but no one would listen to her.

CHAPTER 4

Sunday morning was bright but cold. Rain switched on the electric fire in the living room and huddled near it in her dressing gown while she downed the day's first cup of coffee. The curtains were open so she had a clear view of the square. A handful of leaves rattled by in a chill breeze, and the black labrador investigated something curious in a gutter.

Then a man came into sight, an elderly moustached figure in a tracksuit jogging along the far side of the square. When he reached the end of it he turned the right angle and jogged towards the row of houses where Withy Cottage stood. Rain recognized him then as the General, the bad-tempered rider of the bad-tempered grey horse at the meet. Hadn't Robin Woodley said he lived next door?

The General confirmed it by coming to a halt on the pavement outside the next house and groping in a pocket for his door key. Hampton House was much grander than the rest of the row, possibly the most elegant house in the village but it was hard to say. Its creamy Georgian facade might be a facelift and the interior could prove a disappointment.

The General found his key but was in no hurry to be indoors. He stood and looked approvingly around him. Some drifting leaves came to rest against his foot and he steered them neatly across the pavement until they toppled over the kerb. He took satisfaction from his successful manoeuvre. Then the breeze tore at them and they scampered across the cobbles and away.

Today the General did not look bad tempered at all. He was quite pleased, in fact. His cheeks were a little pink with the coldness of the morning and the exercise but he looked very fit and relaxed. Then he made up his mind to it, moved out of sight and Rain heard the thud of a heavy front door.

She planned her own day around the Sunday papers. She would put a casserole in the oven for her evening meal and that would warm the cottage while it cooked. In the late afternoon she might light the log fire.

But first she had to buy the papers and there was another errand she wanted to get over quickly. She pulled on cord jeans and a warm colourful sweater, swung her bag on to her shoulder and went in search of the newspapers.

They were not sold in the village shop. A child playing outside a house told her a cottage near the church handled them. That was convenient, she wanted to go that way. A man coming down the cottage path was already glancing through his *Sunday Mirror*. Rain didn't have to ask him; he immediately told her she'd find the papers in a conservatory tacked on the back of the cottage.

The selection was slight. Nether Hampton went in for the popular Sundays rather than the heavies but there were several copies of the *Sunday Telegraph*. She bought one, dropping the right change into a plastic foodbox. There was no one to serve her. Joining the street again she continued away from Withy Cottage and crossed the road to the church.

St Michael's slumped lazily among its tip-tilted tombstones. A backdrop of autumnal trees on a rise, which Rain now knew hid the castle, dwarfed its low grey tower. Centuries of drizzle, borne on the soft west winds, had weathered stonework. The clock face had suffered the same way. From a distance it was strangely blotched. Close to, faded blues, reds and yellows of the original finish were apparent.

There was just one gate from the road into the church-yard. Its other exit was on to Widow's Walk, the footpath that led to the castle, but no gate hung here. Posts survived, but someone had long ago taken the iron gate away.

A handful of graves were extremely neat, with fresh flow-ers in containers designed for the job. More were kept just reasonably tidy and had flowers thrust into metal jugs and other improvised holders. Jam jars were popular, and in the corner where the vestry jutted from the bulk of the building some spare jars clustered. Like Nether Hampton itself, St Michael's was no tourist confection. It was neither suspi-ciously trim nor regrettably neglected.

The scene was made of odd angles. The churchyard was an irregular shape, cut short on one side because its high wall flowed beside a stream, elongated in another direction as it stretched towards the castle. The road and flanking proper-ties cramped it at other points. The church lay askew of the short broad path from the iron gate and the village street. And from this path the slender route to the gateless gateway shot off at a tangent. The general crookedness was much of St Michael's charm, but any artist who sketched it would stand accused of exaggeration and, worse, of failing to grasp perspective.

A pair of grey wagtails flashing yellow along the worn gravestones were Rain's only company. She was too early for the only morning service, and she was glad to have the place to herself. In the church porch she found what she had come for, the electoral roll.

There were two pages of it, the parish being quite sparse. Nether Hampton people were listed first, the surrounding hamlets came after in alphabetical order. The Chidgeys were among the first of the Nether Hampton names. Rain tucked her newspaper under her arm and ran her finger down the list.

There were seven Chidgeys including, to her surprise, Wayne of the green hair. She had not imagined he was old enough. Doris and Alfred John of the same address were presumably his parents. They all lived at Mill Cottage in Mill Lane.

Well, that should be simple. The rector, with his enthusiasm for such things, had crowded the rest of the porch with plans of the church and village through the ages. Streets weren't named on his maps but there was one lane with a mill marked. It ran virtually parallel with the village square for a short distance and then veered away towards one of the hamlets.

Rain walked immediately round to Mill Lane. The early sun had gone now and coldness bit so she quickened her pace. There were tits fussing along the hedgerow and cattle mooching in the fields. A horse ambled to a gate to inspect her.

Soon the lane was following a continuation of the stream that skirted the churchyard. There was only one building ahead, the one she had looked towards from the back bedroom of Withy Cottage. It had to be Mill Cottage, there was nothing else there, but it was a charmless Victorian farm cottage and not the one-time mill she had expected.

A sleek brown puppy bounced up and barked the news that Mill Cottage had a visitor. Doris Chidgey came round the back of the house wiping her hands on a torn apron. Rain recognized the square-faced woman from the gathering at the church gate the previous afternoon.

'It's about Adam Hollings . . .' she began.

'You'd best come inside out of this bitter wind.' Mrs Chidgey led her into a low old-fashioned kitchen where the puppy and two cats were reaching an uneasy truce beneath a wooden table littered with the debris of breakfast.

'I'm sorry it's in such a state,' said Mrs Chidgey. She clamped a roughened red hand on the side of a brown teapot. 'Still hot. Would you like a cup?'

Rain thanked her but said no, she wouldn't stop, she just wondered whether Mrs Chidgey knew when Adam Hollings was coming home.

'No, and no more do I know when he went away. He always lets me know but this time he never said a word.' Mrs Chidgey sounded hurt by the slight.

31

'When was it you last saw him?'

'Two months maybe?' She tilted her head and shouted at the ceiling. 'Alf! When were it we saw Mr Hollings?'

There was a muffled roar from upstairs. Doris Chidgey shouted back: 'What?' And the muffled cry came again. 'He'll be down,' she said.

Alf Chidgey thumped down bare wooden stairs and into the kitchen. He was a burly man with baggy trousers and flapping shirt. His hair, uncombed, stuck up spikily from his scalp like an iron-grey version of Wayne's punk look. He nodded a greeting at Rain.

'She's asking about Mr Hollings, Alf,' said his wife.

He sniffed, felt in his trouser pocket for a handkerchief. Didn't find one, and sniffed again. 'What about Mr Hollings?'

Rain said: 'I wondered when he went away and when he's coming back.'

'Ah, well,' said Alf Chidgey, discovering a box of paper tissues on the window sill beside another cat and blowing hard. 'We all wonder about that.'

'Alf!' Doris Chidgey gave him a sharp look. 'All I'm asking you to say is when was it we saw him. You know, that night in the pub. I reckon that's the last time I saw him.'

Alf Chidgey threw his tissue on to the open range. 'Well, that's easy, that is.' He kept them waiting, the centre of attention and timing his moment.

At last: 'The night them Stranglers was playing the Smugglers.'

'Oh yes.' Doris Chidgey was well satisfied.

Rain asked: 'When exactly was that?'

Alf said: 'What day, you mean? The date?'

'Yes,' said Rain, 'the date.'

She had spoiled his triumph. He shook his head dismissively. 'Oh I can't say about dates. But that's when it were.'

'When the Stranglers played the Smugglers?' Rain echoed doubtfully.

'That's what I said.'

Doris Chidgey backed him up. 'Yes, he's right.'

'Is that it, then?' said Alf, looking from his wife to Rain and back.

When they had both assured him it was and thanked him twice he clumped away into another room. The sound of a radio welled up.

Rain said: 'Mrs Chidgey, who are these Stranglers? And Smugglers?'

'Skittlers!' cried Doris Chidgey as though it was an amazing question. She recovered and decided to explain. ''Tis all skittlers round here. The Smugglers is from the Flatner Inn at Stockway and the Stranglers is from the pub at Strangton.'

'I see. And they were playing at . . . ?'

'At the Flatner. That's how I remember, see. I don't go to the pub with him—' a nod in the direction of the distant Alf '—in the normal way, but he said, "Come on," he said, "I'll take you to the Flatner. There's a good match on there tonight."'

'And you saw Adam Hollings there.'

'He was always there. Leastways that's what I'm told. Like I said, I don't go to pubs much.'

Warfare broke out between the cat and the puppy beneath the kitchen table and Doris Chidgey roared at them. When the row subsided, and all she had to contend with was Alf's insistent radio, Rain asked her about Withy Cottage.

Mrs Chidgey said she went in every Friday when Mr Hollings was there, he was a very tidy young man and so once a week was enough. She supposed if there was anything needed doing in between times he did it himself.

'And when he's away? Do you go in then?'

'No, there don't seem much reason. Leastways I don't in the normal way, but this time I didn't know he'd gone, so I suppose I did. What happened, I saw him in the Flatner on the Wednesday and then on the Friday morning I let myself into the cottage and got on with the cleaning.'

Mrs Chidgey grew conspiratorial. 'Well, it never takes me long — just a bit of vacuuming and dusting and a mop over the kitchen and bathroom floors. Sometimes there's a mark on the stove. Now and then I'll do the windows. You know what it is.'

Rain nodded encouragingly. 'So you wouldn't have known when you went in whether he'd gone off on one of his long trips or whether he had just gone shopping?'

Doris Chidgey agreed. She wouldn't have known. Mr Hollings wasn't a man to leave things lying around even when he was there. It made her job so much easier.

'Well then,' said Rain, coaxing her along and hoping to avoid another litany of chores, 'what made you realize he had gone away?'

'It was on the Friday after. In I went again, see, and it was just the same only the letters hadn't been picked up. I don't think he ever had much from the postman, but whatever Fred Stoddens brought him was lying on the doormat waiting for me. I put them on the desk. Three there were.'

She hesitated, looked uncomfortable and then hurried on. 'So what I did then, I went to the front bedroom and I opened that big wardrobe door and had a look. Well, I wouldn't touch his cupboards in the normal way, but I thought if the wardrobe is bare then he's packed his clothes and gone.'

'And it was?'

Mrs Chidgey nodded. 'What he does, when he knows he's going to be away for a bit he sees if he can let the cottage — well, you'd know that, of course. And he locks all his own things away in that cupboard in the bedroom wall. Calls it his wall safe. Mind you, he must have come back at one time because later on I noticed the shutters were closed. Now are you sure you won't have a cup of tea?'

Rain declined again, thanked Mrs Chidgey for her help and prepared to leave. 'There's just one more thing,' she added as they stepped outside. 'How long is he usually away when he goes in the autumn?'

'A month,' said Mrs Chidgey without doubt.

The village was fully awake when Rain got back to Withy Cottage. People clutching newspapers were trailing back from the conservatory. Others were criss-crossing the cobbled square. Elderly women in felt hats and camel coats were walking to church. The sun was making another attempt.

Rain went straight to Adam Hollings's desk and sifted through the papers she had previously tidied. But there was only one unopened letter. It was stamped with the name of his bank branch in Portlet. The postmark was 2 September.

She considered the situation while preparing her casserole and putting it into a low oven. Adam Hollings had now been away two months and that was a month longer than his usual seasonal trip. Mrs Chidgey was only certain he'd gone when she found letters on the doormat. She'd put three of them on the desk, now there was only one unopened. The other letters that were there were all shoved back into torn envelopes, and they were all postmarked well before 2 September.

The sky had darkened and the wind brought raindrops hissing against the kitchen window. It didn't matter, there was sure to be a log fire in the Flatner.

CHAPTER 5

Stockway was a village on the edge of the bay, the Flatner Inn an uninviting pub at one end of it. The most interesting feature was the inn sign which explained its name by a picture of a flat-bottomed craft skimming over the tidal bay.

But if the pub itself was nothing to look at, its view was well worth a visit. The weather had cleared again and sun had won the round. Wind whipped the waters of the estuary and where the tide receded a pebble ridge gleamed blue and pink and ochre.

Hills across the bay were a warm brown, the seaside town beneath them pale as vanilla ice. Small boats jerked upriver and on the Welsh shore windows winked. The stack of the Welsh steelworks was no more significant than a wispily smoking cigarette.

Rain took her sandwich and cider to a window table. The pub was busy. Some well-wrapped families sat in the garden, comparing fossils and pebbles they'd collected from the beach. Indoors, a tweedy group of weekenders argued the merits of the M4 versus the M3 on their headlong dash to the country. Beside them farmers, affecting the shabby dress of the well-to-do, relived the thrills of yesterday's hunt. Two accounted for, and someone — Rain couldn't make out who — had fallen off quite spectacularly.

At the other end of the bar the legitimately shabby were more concerned about the standard of the Smugglers team for next Wednesday than anything else. 'I tell 'ee, there be summat wrong with George,' a balding man was telling the group.

'George'll be sticking up,' someone else insisted.

'George is all right,' said a third and sank his face to his beer.

The balding man defended his opinion. 'I never said he weren't all right, I said there be summat wrong with ee.'

'Ee can give I the sticking up,' offered a tiny man with a very red face. Nobody took up the offer.

The team was giving them anxiety as well as the sticker up. The balding man broke away and consulted a card hanging by the door that said Ladies.

''Tis right,' he called over. And they worried about the crossing out of the name of one of their best men.

Beside the card were pinned photographs of teams and it was natural for any woman on her way to the Ladies to look at them. Rain read the fixture list instead. The Smugglers had taken on the Stranglers at the Flatner on 3 September. The Stranglers, unsurprisingly, had throttled them.

She was recognized as soon as she came back into the bar. A member of the farming set caught her eye and grinned, pausing in the lighting of his pipe. Perhaps in his early forties, he already had the mannerisms of an older man.

'It's Rain Morgan, isn't it? You found the body,' he said erroneously.

She was obliged to join them, to swap the worries of the Smugglers for the murder theories of the farmers. At least it left them little time for earnest questioning about the role of gossip columnists in modern life and dissection of Fleet Street in general.

Amusingly, she was presumed to have a fully developed theory about the murder. She hadn't. Hugo Brand, the pipesmoker, insisted: 'Oh, but you must!' She demurred. Cynthia, his pretty wife, told him not to tease.

Their friend, Caroline Merridge, a solemn lumpish woman clad in riding clothes, bought another round and included Rain without asking. 'Cider, wasn't it?' She thrust a glass at her.

Rain could picture Caroline Merridge, without much alteration, as the horsey schoolgirl she must once have been. She'd stuck with horses when her prettier, less awkward friends had moved on to men and found husbands among the richer farmers. Probably Caroline had always had more rapport with animals than with people, and probably always would. People were what she fitted in around the important matters of life.

Sunday lunchtimes at the Flatner were occasions when the Hugo Brands buttoned on elderly Viyella shirts that had promised never to be quite threadbare enough to throw away, and the Cynthias made themselves bright and fresh in casual wear in coordinating fashionable colours. There were even a few dresses in the bar.

Caroline, in her riding garb, with the mud of a morning's ride on her boots, was refusing to compete. Rain wondered fleetingly what became of the Carolines who were town bred. Without the bolt hole of the stables, what did they do with themselves?

Hugo Brand was speaking again. To tease Cynthia he gave Rain his cheeky grin and demanded to know what had lured her to Nether Hampton: was it the company of a certain archaeologist? Cynthia was, quite reasonably, cross with him. She apologized to Rain. But he had given Rain as neat an opening as she could have wished.

'No, it was Adam Hollings. I'm borrowing his cottage while he's away. I don't suppose any of you know when he's coming back?'

Caroline, just turning from the bar with her own refilled glass, stopped and stared at Rain, her plain face expressionless. Cynthia dropped her eyes to watch the ice melting in her glass. Hugo held his grin, then pulled the pipe from between his teeth and mumbled that they couldn't help. Then, in a firmer tone, went on: 'Nice little cottage. On the square, isn't it?'

'Very nice,' said Rain.

It was much jollier talking about the murder and how hopeless the local police would be at solving it. 'They ought to call in Scotland Yard,' said Caroline, pawing the carpet with a booted foot.

'I think that's losing face, isn't it?' said Hugo. 'They all want to prove they can do it themselves these days.'

Rain murmured something about regional crime squads.

'I suppose we'll be swarming with reporters,' Caroline grumbled.

Cynthia apologized to Rain for her. Caroline retorted: 'Well, Cynthia, I don't mean her. She's not a swarm, is she? It's the swarm I object to.'

As soon as she could Rain left them to it. The tide was well out and the space between the pebble ridge and the foamy edge of the sea was a shining expanse of grey mud. Long-legged birds stepped in their pernickety way over the lambent emptiness.

In the car Rain looked at the map she'd brought from the cottage and found another route back to Nether Hampton. A mile from the village she swung the car into the roadside and climbed a stile on to a footpath. After the smoke and crush of the pub she needed clean air, the feel of leaves beneath her feet.

Trees and shrubs tunnelled her view. Blue tits sang out their piercing warnings that she was coming and there was the faint scent of horses, suggesting a stables somewhere close. She was going in the direction of the castle, but according to the map she could turn off before it and loop back to the car. And on the first leg she could be nosey about Nether Hampton Hall, where Sir James Alcombe lived.

That was a disappointment. The house had been largely rebuilt by an uninspired Victorian architect. There was a short crenellated tower ending in ironwork, some heavy gables and bay windows. The effect was clumsy and ill-proportioned and did not sit happily in the landscape.

She rested on a stile that gave on to a ploughed field and thought what a shame it was. Whatever the house had looked like before the 'improvements' it must have been more handsome than this.

Further on her path forked, the track to the left being the one where she would come out on the return journey. Now she took the right-hand branch and wandered on, spotting fruits, foliage, fungi and all the creeping signs of the season.

She was very close to the castle. The earthworks ringing it were beside her, the stone wall peeped from ivy. And that, she saw, was the tower. She must be on Widow's Walk now.

Definitely not at night, she decided, but in daylight it was innocent enough. If she was not to follow Widow's Walk down into the churchyard she would have to watch out for a path to her left. And there it was, officially a stile but the hedge running up to it was forced apart so that she could step through.

The path now took her along inside the garden of a smart Victorian house which peered at her down the slope of its lawn. There was a verandah, partly enclosed, made for sitting in a basket chair eating cucumber sandwiches and admiring the changing colours of the Quantocks. For all she knew someone did just that.

The dog, when it came, startled her. There was a sudden shrill sound and the chihuahua was bouncing down the lawn. A woman in a purple tweed suit followed, calling: 'Peppy! Here, Peppy!' And to Rain: 'He won't hurt you.'

Rain had not imagined he could. She went to the dog, holding out her hand and talking kindly. The nearer she got the further Peppy retreated, still barking aggressively.

'Did he give you a fright?' the woman asked. She wore an unfashionable amount of make-up, chose an accent that aimed at northern genteel and used it much too loudly. 'He's not used to people taking this path.' She scooped Peppy up into her arms and began purring at him. He stopped barking and quivered with emotion.

'He made me jump, I hadn't noticed him,' Rain said. She stretched out a hand and gently stroked Peppy's head, careful of the molera where the skull would never knit and a pulse throbbed. 'I saw you at the hunt yesterday,' she said ambiguously.

The woman assumed she meant both of them. 'We always watch the horses, don't we, Peppy?' Peppy fixed enormous dark eyes on her. His owner set him down and watched him trot back to the verandah, light as an autumn leaf. Her heavily ringed hands checked her bouffant grey hair. 'My dog has introduced himself, and so must I. I'm Mrs Murray.'

'Rain Morgan.'

'I know. *You* found the body.' It was a popular error.

'Not exactly . . .'

'Do they know yet who it was?' Mrs Murray shuddered slightly, or it may have been a shiver. The sun had gone for the day.

'I'm afraid I don't know. All I know is Robin Woodley found a body.'

'Terrible,' said Mrs Murray. '*Terrible* for him. It could have been *me*. And Peppy. We could have found it. That's where I walk him, you see. Down here, over the lawn, out on to the path, up to the castle and back.'

She laughed. 'I should say that's where *he* walks *me*. Off he goes, always the same way, but at any time that he fancies and I have to follow. Any sort of weather, he's just the same. They're *very* intelligent you know.'

Rain thought it sounded rather stupid. She said: 'You'd have been quite safe. This was inside the castle.'

But Mrs Murray was busy shocking herself. 'Supposing Peppy'd dug it up?'

Rain couldn't think of anything less likely. She was wondering how to reply when Mrs Murray turned the conversation. 'Do you play bridge?'

41

'Bridge? Not for a long time.' Teenage evenings indulging her aunt and friends flickered through her mind.

'I need someone for bridge. Will you come? Tomorrow evening, about eight.'

'Oh, but I'm not very good. I wouldn't want to spoil your evening.'

'It's spoiled if you *don't* come. You're my only hope. Eight o'clock.' And she was thanking Rain and backing away up the slanting lawn.

'All right,' Rain called up to her, laughing. 'You win.'

'I hope so,' said Mrs Murray, triumphant. 'I *hope* so.'

There was another surprise before Rain reached her car. In a barn in a field beside the looping path she came upon a group of lads putting the finishing touches to an elaborate carnival float. They had taken a farm trailer and given it an exotic disguise. Now they were fixing to it the hundreds of lightbulbs that would bring it to life. The lad who was organizing their efforts was Wayne Chidgey, whose green hair was suddenly no more than part of an overall effect. They did not spot her and she passed softly by.

Withy Cottage was warm with the scent of cooking. She lit her log fire and had a lazy evening with the newspaper and then a book.

It was a cosy, selfish sort of time. She rang Oliver once, but the phone was engaged and she didn't bother again. Instead she helped herself to some of Adam Hollings's whisky, tossed another log on to the fire and went back to her novel. Tomorrow evening was going to be unmitigated social disaster. She deserved this solitary indulgence.

The next day passed quietly. She bought Adam a replacement bottle so she need not feel guilty about dipping into his. She pottered about the cottage, dusting and tidying. Why was it one never remembered what a mess an open fire made? Not just ash, but the dust that gently smothered a room.

She washed some underwear and a blouse and carried them into the garden to hang out. A line stretched from a pole that supported a woody wintering clematis. An iron

42

hook thrust into a high grey stone wall took the other end. Wooden clothes pegs swung from the line.

That was odd, she thought, for someone as meticulously tidy as Adam Hollings. She would have expected a neat bundle in a drawer somewhere. But was inconsistency really ever odd? Perhaps not. During the silent task of hanging out the clothes, voices began on the other side of the wall.

'Oh, there you are. I'm just mulching the border, I didn't expect you back yet. No, it's all right, I've finished now.' A woman. Upper-class accent. The General's wife.

A man's rumbling tones, approaching. The woman again. 'I hope you didn't accept, Frank. You know we can't. There's bridge tonight.'

'Damn, is it tonight?'

'Yes, Monday. It's always Monday because there's nothing she wants to see on the television on Mondays.'

'You're bitching. You are always bitching about her. I don't know why you go.'

She said patiently: 'Yes you do, Frank. It's because there's nothing else to do. And it's not bitching. She said it herself.'

There was a pause and then he said: 'Why don't you check with her? She might not have a fourth. She didn't last time and we just sat there looking at each other.'

'She's got a fourth. That woman staying next door. She rang me to say so.'

The General's tone brightened. 'Well, that's all right then.'

Ironically: 'You would think so, Frank.'

Defensively: 'I only meant she'd be interesting. And she can tell us about the murder.'

'They haven't said it was murder, have they?'

Their voices drifted off, arguing the unlikelihood of anyone but a murder victim being buried in such a way.

CHAPTER 6

Rain kept watch on the iron gates of Laurel House across the square. She did not want to be there first and sat poised to leave Withy Cottage once she knew the General and his wife had already arrived.

Exactly at eight she heard them coming out of Hampton House. Withy Cottage resounded with the heavy closing of their front door. The General, in a smooth greenish tweed suit and woollen tie, took his wife's arm and led her over the cobbles. His wife's hair looked newly waved and she wore elegant high-heeled shoes. Bridge with Mrs Murray was apparently something to smarten oneself up for.

The door of Laurel House was not visible from the square. Its iron gates were set in a wall — where once, surely, there had been iron railings instead — and visitors had to veer left across a tiny courtyard to gain the porch. Laurel House had been designed to take advantage of its Quantock view, and turned its back on Nether Hampton.

Rain allowed good time for the General and his wife to be admitted. Then she left Withy Cottage. Her knitted dress and coloured shoes and tights would have to do. She had packed more formal clothes, because one never knew, but she had decided bridge with Peppy's mistress hardly qualified for them.

The door sprang open as soon as the bell struck up with a Yorkshire folk tune. Rain expected Mrs Murray but instead an anxious-faced woman in a white apron welcomed her.

Rain was taken through a carpeted hall and into a large sitting room with a wide glass door which, in warmer weather, would be opened on to the covered part of the verandah. There were rose pink nylon-velvet curtains but they were not drawn across the door.

Mrs Murray, in peacock blue silk with a hint of mink trimming at her throat, came forward in greeting, beringed hands outstretched. She was effusive. The General's wife smiled a smile that did not reach as far as her eyes. Two men rose politely, the General and Sir James Alcombe. Rain wondered which of the four people greeting her was not going to play and how the spare member of the party was to be occupied.

The woman in the apron was told: 'Jessie, pour Miss Morgan a sherry, would you?' She obliged and then slid thankfully away.

'We may all call you Rain, mayn't we?' assumed Mrs Murray, easing into a reproduction Chippendale chair covered in more rose pink nylon velvet.

The General was eager to be 'Frank', Sir James Alcombe suggested 'Jimmy', and the General's wife offered 'Edwina'. Mrs Murray said nothing at all, leaving Rain to deduce that she expected to be Mrs Murray.

And so Rain saw them all together, and for a few hours she became one of them. In the weeks ahead she would switch her mind back to that evening, rerun her mental pictures of the room, the people and their poses.

She would listen over and over to the chit-chat as she remembered it, probing a sentence here, questioning a word there, listening for what she might at the time have missed. She would hold their gestures and their faces in a freeze frame to study them meticulously.

And all the time she would be studying not the others but herself. She was on holiday, her professional caution was switched off. And it ought not to have been. Perhaps — and at the heart of it this was her concern — perhaps if she had reserved enough caution she might have avoided some of what was to come.

But when Jessie poured the sherry and Frank, Edwina and Jimmy gave her their first names, and Mrs Murray, in her peacock silk, sank on to her counterfeit chair, Rain saw no omens.

She merely thought that there was nothing so strange as a room full of strangers. The reasons for the flickering expressions were a secret, the by-play and the interweaving of relationships were unexplained. Familiarity would smooth all that away and each appearance was but another aspect of a labelled subject, an addition to a fund of information and opinion. That was why first impressions were so important. Things were then as they would never be again.

Robin Woodley had given Rain his view of the four when she had her first glimpse of them on the morning of the hunt. Oliver, if he had seen them, would have gone further, rejecting subtlety for the broader smile. But that was his job: find the absurdity and exaggerate it. Rain's business was to question, to look beneath the most confidently worn mask. And she failed.

Frank Corning did not entirely match Robin's hopeful categorization. Generals a-plenty retire to country villages and emerge camouflaged as chairmen of councils, from parish to county level. An air of knowledgeable seriousness impresses the locals who are curiously willing to assume that outsiders with a military background know what is best for them.

General Frank Corning appeared foolish and frivolous with his passion for jogging, especially as it was no longer the extremely fashionable activity it had been a few years earlier. Worse, he was an unforgivably poor seat on a horse.

The General was not in control, and when he was not in control he covered his inadequacy with displays of bad temper. Not, then, a man to go over the top with. But for an evening's company? That could be quite a different ordeal.

In contrast Edwina Corning was the cool, organized type. If she were to run the village fête there would be utter confidence in her ability to get it right. But Edwina Corning was not one to dabble among the white elephants and the bring-and-buys. All that was a little beneath her. She confined her support to a purchase of jam and the gift of a pair of the General's retired cavalry twills for the church sale.

Where Edwina Corning was restrained in manner, Mrs Murray flowed freely. Her bubbling, emphatic speech insisted to visitors that they were having a good time even when, not so very deep down, they knew otherwise. Provided she had everyone's undiluted attention *she* would enjoy herself. Having moved to Nether Hampton she was ruthlessly becoming part of it.

A total stranger wandering into that sitting room would have assumed that Edwina Corning was Lady Alcombe. There was an empathy between the General's wife and Sir James. There was the same quiet confidence, the assurance of the well-born that, even in egalitarian times, allowed a class to exchange shibboleths of gesture and thought.

Sir James, tallish with thinning sandy hair, was a disappointment as an aristocrat at even the most meagre level. At the hunt there had been a certain authority about him and perhaps horses were as much his life as they were Caroline Merridge's. Here, dressed in a pale suit, sipping medium dry sherry with his neighbours, he was an insignificant figure.

Peppy came and sprang on to Mrs Murray's lap, her cue to introduce speculation about how dreadful it would have been if Peppy had dug up the body. Mrs Murray turned her immaculately coiffured grey head to Rain who shared a sofa with Frank Corning.

'This body,' she said with relish, 'is the most *thrilling* thing that's happened here for *years*.'

This forced a laugh from the others. 'Well, in *my* time, anyway,' she qualified.

'And how long is that?' Rain asked, hoping to learn about Mrs Murray instead of about Peppy's prowess as a terrier. Frank Corning was already saying that chihuahuas were Mexican dogs who dug themselves burrows to get out of the sun.

'Four years?' Mrs Murray consulted the others.

'Must be,' said Frank Corning, quick to agree.

'Is it as long as that?' asked Sir James.

They all assured him it was. Sir James shook his head, unconvinced. He was standing with his back to the elaborate Victorian fireplace, but Mrs Murray had central heating and had switched that on instead.

'Don't you *remember*, Jimmy?' she said. 'I was here for the night of the big storm? When my elm tree came down?'

'I remember my barn blowing away,' he said. She looked disappointed.

'Isn't it funny,' said Edwina Corning without humour, 'how one always remembers things by disasters. Droughts. Storms. That sort of thing.'

'And murders,' her husband said enthusiastically.

The bridge table was waiting. Soon they were grouped around it. It was the General who did not play. He hovered near the fireplace — somehow one could not hover near a radiator — and then took up a book and flopped into a chair. The cards were cut and dealt by Sir James.

'You'd better make a good fist of it, Rain,' the General called over to her. 'Adam will never forgive you if you don't.'

'Nor will *I*,' laughed Mrs Murray, whom Rain was partnering.

'Adam Hollings?' Rain showed more surprise than she would have chosen.

'Yes,' said Mrs Murray happily.

'You are taking his place all round,' Edwina Corning said quietly, studying her cards.

Rain played as badly as she had feared. Mrs Murray managed to be kind about it.

The General constantly interrupted with remarks that had nothing to do with the play. Part of the time he read pieces at them from the book he had picked up. Presumably he was forgiven this irritation because for the rest of the time he refilled their glasses and let the indecisive Peppy in and out of the room, in and out of the garden.

There was a respite at about nine o'clock when the anxious-looking Jessie came in pushing a trolley bearing snacks. The General began to fill a plate, without waiting for an invitation to do so. A telephone rang across the hall. Mrs Murray excused herself and left the room. Rain got up from the table, Edwina Corning and Sir James lingered.

'Rather good, this,' said the General, carving a hunk off the slab of cheese. 'Local.'

Rain sounded interested. The General said: 'You ought to expect it in Somerset, but you're lucky to get it.' He gave what he intended as a mischievous grin. 'Of course, if you know *where* . . .' The grin jerked into a wink, the white moustache bobbed.

As an afterthought he offered to cut a piece for Rain and she waited while he selected the exact spot where the knife should cream into the Cheddar. Not, naturally, where it would lop off such an impolitely gigantic piece as it had lopped off for him. Yet neither must it be too scant beside his own portion.

He reached his compromise and down came the blade. 'Try that, my dear. Always have some more if you like it, eh?'

While he was going through the ritual of describing the choice of biscuits, Rain was tuning in to the conversation behind her at the card table. It was audible but unclear. If she had not seen in the mirror above the fireplace that Edwina Corning had checked that she was unobserved before she spoke, then Rain would not have wondered.

Edwina Corning was leaning towards Sir James. 'Too bad of her, Jimmy,' Rain heard her say.

Sir James concurred with a weary nod. 'But if she won't, she won't. I can do no more than ask.'

'A senseless piece of selfishness,' Edwina Corning said. A pause. She added: 'If I thought *my* asking her would help . . .'

'Oh no, no,' he said quickly. 'I'm sure it wouldn't. I will write again.'

Edwina Corning did not push her offer, glad enough not to have it accepted. She was about to say something more but Sir James was getting up and suggesting they join Rain and Frank.

'C'mon,' the General called to them. 'It'll all be gone.' He cut himself just a slender second helping of the local Cheddar.

'I'm trying to train him to leave some for others,' Edwina Corning said with a humourless smile.

'Actually, I don't know how you do it,' said Sir James to the General. 'Always a fair appetite and not a spare inch to show for it.'

The General, oblivious of any admonition, beamed. 'Exercise,' he said. 'Keeps you fit, keeps you trim. Eat what you like if you take exercise.'

'You jog every day?' Rain asked.

'Every morning, some evenings. You see, it's the perfect exercise. Gentle rhythm, fresh air. You ought to come along.'

Edwina Corning looked at him in wonder.

Rain said: 'A kind offer, but no thank you. I get as much exercise as I want in the morning just getting out of bed.' She correctly judged that was just the sort of banal response that was required.

Mrs Murray flurried back into the sitting room. '*Well*, now, are you all helping yourselves? Good, that's the idea. Sorry to have been *so* long, leaving you to it. But your *friends* are the people who put up with your bad manners, that's what I always say. Rain, dear, have they told you to try this cheese?'

Rain complimented her on the cheese and said she was already planning to take some back to London if someone would tell her where to buy it.

The General, about to renew his attack on the cheese, cried: 'Aha, that would be telling!'

Edwina Corning gave him her surprised look again. 'Really, Frank? Don't we all just go up to the dairy at Stockway and ask for it?'

Her husband coloured, his moustache quivered, his hand tightened on the handle of the knife. Mrs Murray wrested the knife from him and cut herself a generous wedge. 'Well, I'm sure *I* don't,' she said brightly. 'I always send Jessie.' She laughed loudly at her own indulgence.

'Does Jessie live in?' Rain asked, looking for safer ground. The difficulty of finding servants in Nether Hampton might just be safe.

'Heavens no,' Mrs Murray said, still laughing. 'There's just me here. A bit big you might say for one woman but I'm happy here and it's what you're used to, that's what I always say. Jessie comes each day to clean and on the evenings when I'm entertaining. Then she goes home. She lives down by the church. Her husband does the newspapers.'

'And talking of newspapers,' said the General, finishing a mouthful of cheese, 'We have heard not a word from you yet about the *Daily Post*.'

Until they went back to the card table the talk was all about newspapers. The Cornings announced themselves as *Daily Telegraph* readers and Sir James admitted he'd always been a *Times* man. Mrs Murray, pressed, said she didn't take a paper regularly but when she bought one it was likely to be the *Telegraph*. Or the *Daily Post*. Rain was convinced Mrs Murray was an *Express* reader, and that any *Guardians* that went into Withy Cottage had better be smuggled there under plain cover.

As they seated themselves at the card table again, Peppy came whimpering and fussing. Mrs Murray said he wanted to go for his walk and wasn't it bothersome that he didn't have a routine about these matters as other dogs did? He would be quite put out for the rest of the evening because she was not going to take him out now. She turned down Frank Corning's offer to walk Peppy and said she would just let him out into the garden for a few minutes.

To Rain she said: 'Come with me.' It was said in a tone that didn't allow for refusal. Rain followed obediently down the passage. 'I haven't shown you the cloaks,' said Mrs Murray, teetering on high heels towards the rear of the house. 'You'll think I'm a *very* poor hostess. Leaving you all that time I was on the phone, and forgetting to show you where to wash your hands.'

At the end of the passage, next to a back door where Peppy waited expectantly, was a brown-painted door with a china plaque which said Cloakroom in italic handwriting decked with sprays of painted flowers. The back door was duly opened for Peppy. Rain, left with no choice in the matter, went into the cloakroom.

She did not want to use it and passed the requisite amount of time looking at the decor instead. The spare roll of paper was tucked coyly under a knitted doll with a flounced skirt in turquoise and pink. The wall tiles were pink and the WC and washbasin brown. There was a thick brown carpet but the pink was picked up again in a fluffy mat around the base of the WC and a matching cover on the seat.

And then, through the frosted-glass window behind the WC, she saw a movement. She thought Mrs Murray was indoors, surely she could hear her moving about the passage? Rain flushed the WC, switched off the light and then quickly lifted the metal arm at the base of the window and swung the window open.

It was dark outside but she was aware that someone was there, pressed against the wall near the window. As she did not know the layout of the Laurel House garden she could not guess which direction the figure might flee. She could wait a long time at the open window for a glimpse of his departure only to find he had made off in the opposite direction.

Then Peppy began to whimper. 'What is it, darling?' Mrs Murray called soothingly, her voice approaching down the passage. 'Mummy opened the door for you but you *wouldn't* go out. It's no use sulking, I can't take you for a walk now.'

Rain had to leave the window then and go into the passage. She said: 'Please, don't open the back door. There's someone out there.'

Mrs Murray froze, clutched melodramatically at the mink about her throat. '*Who?*' she demanded.

Rain told her what she had seen and sensed. Mrs Murray whisked Peppy into her arms and backed down the passage. 'Oh my *God*,' she said. 'Come *away* from there. I'll fetch Jimmy.'

'No, I'll stay near the window. No one will try to come in now, but I might just get a peep at him.'

As the noise of the cistern subsided Rain thought she heard the soft thud of footsteps over the sloping lawn, but by then there was so much noise indoors that she could not be sure. General Corning, followed by Sir James Alcombe, Edwina Corning and Mrs Murray, was marching down the passage.

'Where is he?' the General asked with all the menace of a man leading a lynch mob. He was speaking in a stage whisper and had made them switch off all the lights.

'I don't know,' Rain whispered back. 'I think he was round here, to the left of the cloakroom window.' It was not easy to gesticulate effectively now all the lights were switched off.

'Then in that case if we dash out of the back door we should catch him. Someone could lean out of the cloakroom window and grab him if he tries to escape to the right.' Absurd, and he was in deadly earnest.

'A pincer action, dear?' said Edwina Corning unkindly.

The General ignored her. 'Jimmy,' he ordered, 'you take the cloakroom. I'll bound out of the back door and pursue.'

Sir James hesitated. 'Now look, Frank . . . He could be armed. Or anything.'

'Just stick your arm out of the window, there's a good chap.'

Mrs Murray and Peppy whimpered unhappily in the background. Rain said tentatively: 'We don't know that he's still there.'

The General disregarded that. He whispered, 'Into the cloakroom with you, Jimmy. Arm right out to block escape.'

Sir James and Edwina Corning, standing close together, exchanged glances. 'Well, let us hope you don't get a broken arm,' she said softly. Sir James went meekly into the cloakroom.

The General motioned everyone to silence, inched to the back door, grasped the handle, turned it soundlessly, and shot into the dark beyond with a whoop.

Everyone leaped in astonishment. Peppy began to bark. Mrs Murray said: 'Oh my *God*.' Rain used a hand to stifle spluttering laughter. Edwina Corning buried her face in her hands but she was not laughing.

There was a bang, a scuffling, a commotion outside. 'I believe I've got him,' shouted an amazed Sir James from his vantage point at the cloakroom window.

'Let go, you fool!' The General sounded as though he were being throttled. Sir James let go of the General's throat.

They regrouped in the sitting room. The General's woollen tie was a twisted rag. There was a reddening patch on his forehead where he had run slap into the open cloakroom window.

Edwina Corning stood coolly elegant near the food trolley and casually helped herself to titbits while the others assessed the situation. Mrs Murray sat with Peppy on her peacock silk lap, both of them wide-eyed and nervous.

'I think we should call the police,' said Frank Corning, smoothing his moustache.

'Send for reinforcements, dear?' threw in Edwina. She popped another Cheesy Shape into her mouth.

'Can they do much about a prowler, though?' asked Sir James doubtfully. 'The fellow's gone and by the time they get here from town he could be miles away.'

'What do *you* think, Rain?' Mrs Murray asked. 'After all, he's *your* prowler.'

Rain did not feel at all proprietorial about him. She said lamely: 'The police might find footprints in the flowerbed. Or something.' And she pictured the polite patience of a couple of policemen sent to investigate a possible prowler that no one was sure they had seen or heard.

'In that case,' said the General with inspiration, 'we might as well look ourselves.'

'Oh *no*,' gasped Mrs Murray histrionically. 'Don't go outside. He might still be around. You could be hurt.'

'We have got to go outside at some stage,' said Sir James. 'Can't spend the rest of the night here.' He was with the General, now that it was certain that whoever had been lurking was long gone. He set off down the passage. This time the General brought up the rear.

Rain, Edwina Corning and Mrs Murray stayed in the sitting room. Mrs Murray was still shaken, although in time, of course, the adventure would become one of the thrilling things that had happened since she moved to Nether Hampton.

'Would you feel safer, Joan, if the police were to check?' Edwina asked. 'As Jimmy says, we do all have to go home this evening and then you will be on your own.'

'I'm used to being on my own, that doesn't frighten me. I've been widowed five years and that's plenty long enough to get used to being on your own. Peppy's here — he'll soon let me know if anyone comes near the house again. Won't you, my little precious?' She sank her face to her little precious who had circled three times on her lap and begun to doze.

'Yes, he's very alert,' Rain said, remembering how he had flown across the lawn at her on her walk. And how he had come to them at the card table and told them he had heard someone outside. The trouble was that his messages were garbled. 'There's someone breaking into the house' had come over as 'I want to go for a walk.' As guard dogs went, he didn't inspire confidence.

'You must be very careful, Joan,' Edwina was saying seriously. 'If you ever have any suspicions telephone us — at any time — and I will send Frank over.'

Sir James and Frank Corning came back to the sitting room. 'Was there anything?' Rain asked, half hoping there was. If not, it was only a matter of time before everyone concluded she had imagined the whole business and she was dismissed as a neurotic.

Sir James said: 'Footprints? Yes, lots of footprints. In the border. Under the cloakroom window. Couldn't be clearer.'

Relieved, she followed up with: 'What sort of shoes?'

'Men's, about size tens.'

They all looked at the General's muddy size tens.

CHAPTER 7

The card table was ignored for what remained of the evening. None of the players was either particularly good or particularly keen. The diversions of a local murder and a local prowler held much more for them. They settled back among Mrs Murray's cushions and talked about such things instead.

Then Mrs Murray insisted on making them coffee. Jessie had gone home and so Rain was invited to help. Edwina Corning offered, but she was rejected.

The kitchen was large and lavish. Its fitted units were from one of the most expensive solid wooden ranges on the market. All the latest notions in equipment had been incorporated. But where Adam Hollings had selected carefully for Withy Cottage, Mrs Murray had simply bought one of everything that came in her chosen colour, green. She wanted Rain with her to show it off.

'*So* important, I always say, to have a good kitchen. And this *is* a good kitchen. It was one of the first things I had done when I moved here.' Mrs Murray was posing amidst the kitchen units and gleaming appliances like a woman in a television commercial.

'I said to the architect, 'George,' I said, 'what you must give me is a *wonderful* kitchen. That is my *absolute* priority.' And the pet did it, didn't he?'

Rain agreed that George had indeed come up trumps. 'You enjoy cooking, do you?' she asked, making conversation as Mrs Murray touched a drawer and it slid soundlessly open and gave up coffee spoons.

'Cooking?' Mrs Murray sounded vague. 'Well, it's only me, isn't it? Jessie does my main meal when she's here so I've only got to warm it up in the evening. Or I get a little something for myself. So easy these days, isn't it? As I was saying to Jessie only the other day, there isn't anything now, not *anything* you can't get frozen.'

Rain supposed not. She followed Mrs Murray's glance to a tall stainless-steel freezer that would have looked more appropriate in a morgue. Mrs Murray went to its twin, a fridge, and fetched a bottle of milk. Before the door swung shut Rain glimpsed a near-empty interior where a few packages were arranged like *objêts* on the shelves.

Mrs Murray thrust the milk bottle at her. 'You could put that in a jug,' she said, indicating a glass-fronted wall cupboard with imitation lead lights. Rain obeyed.

She made flattering sounds about Laurel House and Mrs Murray's expenditure on it, and then asked about Mrs Murray's previous home. She could imagine it fairly well, she thought. There would be the same eagerness to spend money, believing she was aiming for good quality and safe good looks. And then the same inability not to spoil the effect by overdoing it with tasteless frippery.

Mrs Murray said she had lived 'in the North', her husband had been 'in property', and her previous house had been 'a very grand modern one'. She whisked open a wooden door from one bank of cupboards. She lifted out a jar of instant coffee and flicked the door effortlessly shut again. Rain carried the laden tray back up the passage.

The other three were still talking about the prowler. 'Putting my money on young Chidgey,' said the General. 'Just the sort of thing he'd do, snooping around frightening old ladies.' His moustache juddered with disapproval.

Mrs Murray stiffened. Edwina Corning put in: 'And Generals.'

Sir James said: 'He's still unemployed, I suppose?'

'Good lord, yes,' the General replied. 'Work wouldn't suit that young layabout.'

Rain asked whether there was much work available locally for youngsters like Wayne Chidgey. She was told there was not much available for anyone.

'All he ever does, apart from snooping about, is work on that float they're building for the carnival,' General Corning went on. He fixed a stern look on Mrs Murray. 'You want to tell the police, Joan, that your prowler was quite obviously Wayne Chidgey.'

Edwina said quickly: 'I'm sure the police would be very interested in your theory, Frank, but the only evidence they would find would be your footprints. You have no reason to accuse Chidgey.'

Sir James was nodding, apparently in agreement with her. Before he could speak, Corning was in with: 'Don't need a reason, the very fact he's who he is is good enough for me.' He laughed loudly at his own preposterousness.

Soon Sir James was saying he must get home. Mrs Murray tried to persuade him to stay on. She caught Edwina Corning's eye, enlisting her help.

Edwina rose and said: 'We must be off, too.' Her husband made no move, but Sir James was on his feet. Mrs Murray was very obviously anxious to be rid of her other guests and keep Sir James to herself. Equally obviously Sir James knew that.

In the event they all left together, Sir James leading the way over the little courtyard and on to the village square where his car waited. There was no one else around. The Cornings and Rain set off together across the square, silently. Then the General threw back his shoulders and strode ahead, jingling his front door key in his pocket.

Edwina Corning did not speak until she and Rain said goodnight on the pavement outside Hampton House. Frank Corning had gone straight in and left the door wide open.

Electric light showed Rain a well-proportioned hall with gold and white wallpaper and a gold and white Regency-striped chaise longue. At least that bit of Hampton House lived up to its imposing facade.

Edwina Corning looked from her own spacious home to Withy Cottage crunched up beside it. 'It's quite strange about Adam Hollings, you know,' she said. And went indoors.

Rain phoned Oliver at once. She needed to share with someone the comedy of the evening, and it was precisely the kind of occasion Oliver would relish. He was cheerfully good humoured, delighted to hear her. He'd rung twice earlier, he said. They laughed and joked about Rain's tale.

At last she asked after the office but all he had to tell her was gloom. He'd been for a drink with Tom, but any idea he'd had of providing a bright interlude in the misery was dispelled half-way through the first pint. Rain heard herself warning him not to become involved, there was nothing he could do. Exactly, of course, what he had been telling her for weeks.

'I'm afraid it's the Nether Hampton air,' she apologized. 'It's making me heartless.'

He still did not know how soon he might be able to join her. She had begun to miss him but did not say so. They rang off.

Next morning she woke early with Edwina Corning's parting words echoing in her mind. She was already translating Adam Hollings's absence into his 'disappearance', an altogether more ominous and intriguing speculation.

The day was grey and damp. She crouched by the electric fire in the living room and watched the General jog home — red tracksuit, white running shoes — across the square.

Rain planned to spend her day around the village. There was no point in driving off in search of scenery when the October sky pressed against dull earth.

She went first to buy a paper. The *Daily Post* had not reached the village and *Guardians* would have to be ordered. But there was a lingering copy of the local paper published the previous Wednesday. And so, never able to resist the more old-fashioned weeklies, she bought the *West Somerset Advertiser*.

A glimpse inside promised her all the minutiae of local life, including a page devoted to such newsworthy items as the winning of the handicrafts competitions at the Women's Institute meetings and the appointment of officers at the luncheon clubs. The appeal for the average reader was that he knew all this already. For the visitor from London it was reassuring that this sort of thing went resolutely on and was considered important.

Next she went to the village post office and store for writing paper and envelopes and a few postcard scenes of the village. These featured the square with the Huntsman prominent to one side, Hampton House resplendent on the other and a sliver of Withy Cottage visible.

The post office was crowded and the motherly woman who ran it was singlehanded, darting from the shop counter to serve behind the post office grille and back again. While Rain was paying for her cards and discovering she had to queue again for her stamps, Sir James Alcombe came in.

They exchanged a brief and friendly greeting and he joined the docile women waiting for the postmistress to switch her attention back to postal orders and stamps. Rain was several places behind him in the queue so they did not speak again. She listened to the chit-chat around her, every-day stuff about the weather and so on, and then she heard the postmistress saying deferentially: 'Good morning, Sir James. Keeping well, are you?'

'Yes indeed, thank you, Mrs Wren.'

'Stamps, is it?'

'Yes, please. Half a dozen second class and I also want to send a letter to France so I shall need a stamp for that.' His voice was curiously loud, especially as there was no indication that Mrs Wren's hearing was lacking.

Mrs Wren told him how much the stamp for France cost, what the others came to, did the addition and he handed over the money. He paused on the way out of the shop to put the stamps into a wallet. There were muttered good mornings from others in the queue and then he was gone.

The women in the shop looked after him. There were sympathetic murmurs. 'A stamp for France, Else,' said one, nodding her head knowingly. 'He still writes to France, then.'

''Tis regular,' said another. The women bobbed and shuffled like hens who had scratched up something interesting from the day. 'Mavis'll tell you,' said the second woman tipping her head towards Mrs Wren. 'He writes regular to France.' The others digested this information with surprise except for the two or three who were at pains to show it was old news to them.

With her purchases in her shoulder bag Rain went to Laurel House. The worried-looking Jessie opened the door and asked her to wait in the hall. Mrs Murray was sitting with Peppy on her lap in a morning room and there she stayed until Rain was brought to her.

'My *dear*,' said Mrs Murray with a sweeping gesture at a chair, 'how *nice* to see you.' She nodded at a hovering Jessie who went for coffee. 'And *now*, let me tell you that you are not my *first* visitor today.'

'Sir James Alcombe,' Rain guessed accurately.

'So kind of him, don't you think? Driving all that way just to see that a poor nervous old woman was safe after that *dreadful* experience last night.'

Rain reflected that the drive from Nether Hampton Hall was all of a mile and a half and that Mrs Murray could not seriously wish to be considered poor or nervous or old. Certainly she had not when Frank Corning had clumsily insisted on Wayne Chidgey's penchant for frightening old ladies. Rain said it was very good of Sir James.

Coffee came. Rain explained that she, too, had come to see that Mrs Murray was well and Mrs Murray protested that of course she was, everybody was being so *kind* but really what had there been to it after all?

'I also,' said Rain, moving swiftly on, 'wanted to ask you about Adam Hollings.'

That subject was greeted with less alacrity. Mrs Murray was drinking in the crooked-little-finger style. She paused, the cup half-way to her mouth. 'Adam?' she asked vaguely.

'Yes. I'd like to know when he's coming back. You see, the arrangements for my staying in his house are rather flimsy. I don't know him, he's the cousin of a friend. If I could find out when he is coming home, I would know how long I can stay here.'

'Oh, I shouldn't worry about *that*. Oh no. Adam will be back whenever he's ready.' Her free hand waved the topic away.

'I thought if I could find out where he has gone I could ask him when he plans to return.'

'You might, yes you might.' Mrs Murray sipped, set the cup down, the little finger relaxed.

'So . . . do you know where he is?'

'*Me*? What ever makes you think *I'd* know?'

'Bridge. If he is your regular partner on your weekly bridge evenings, then surely he would have said something about his plans to go away?'

Mrs Murray smoothed her hair while she thought about that. Her fingers, even in the morning, were knobbed with chunky rings. Three gold bracelets rattled on her wrist.

She shook her head sadly. 'I'm sorry, Rain. I don't remember Adam telling me where he was going and he didn't know how long he would be.'

'So he did tell you he was going?' Now she was getting somewhere.

Mrs Murray abandoned her vague look. The eyes narrowed. 'Everybody knows he's gone, *everybody*.'

Rain got no more from her. She might have pushed just a little but Peppy chose that moment to demand to be let into the garden. Rain decided she might as well leave and asked to be allowed to go over the lawn to join the castle path.

'You're *not* going up there,' Mrs Murray said with a shudder.

'No, I'm going to look at the church.' She turned back once to wave. Mrs Murray stood on the verandah watching her, while Peppy inspected a chrysanthemum.

Whichever direction a visitor took to St Michael's he dropped down to it. Its position below the castle rise made it appear smaller than it was. A quirk of fate had cheated it of a handsome Somerset tower of traceried stone and its stubby plain tower was a poor substitute.

Once inside, disappointment vanished. The Norman interior was cavernous and richly embellished with monuments and carved bench ends — a local tradition it *had* enjoyed. The chubby rector, the Reverend Clifford Hadley — red face beneath white hair and a candidate for anyone's Father Christmas — was there and showed Rain the best St Michael's had to offer.

They came to the grand monuments to earlier occupants of Nether Hampton Hall. 'Very fine examples, indeed,' purred the rector. 'Do you see how . . .' He stretched a loving hand to the stone cold features of a long ago knight. 'Pevsner is very kind about our monuments.'

They glided on. There were the Alcombe family monuments. 'Not in the same league, sadly,' the rector grieved. 'And, of course, the Alcombes haven't been here long. Less than two hundred years. The property passed to a nephew when the old family ran out of direct heirs. That is what will happen after Sir James's time. An unfortunate little coincidence.'

He shook his head regretfully over the clumsy excesses of the Alcombe memorials. Bulbous marble cherubs, crude and lengthy verse trying for the grandiose, achieving the sentimental.

'If they ever put up pleasing monuments to themselves then they lie in another church in whichever part of the country they came from. Devon? Dorset? I'm afraid I cannot remember which.' He frowned. It was the sort of detail he liked to remember.

Eventually Rain thanked him for the tour, told him how much she had enjoyed reading his history of the village and prepared to leave. She had time enough to spare, the rector probably hadn't. She asked whether he had a service that morning.

'A funeral, at 11.45. I don't know why the forty-five, presumably it suits the undertakers.' They were walking towards the door. 'Emily Parsons, a very old lady. Ninety, or ninety-one. I'm sure she didn't know which herself. A quiet funeral, two or three members of her family, two or three friends.'

He broke off to point out the unadorned wall plaque which announced the passing of an Alcombe. 'Sir James's father,' he said.

'The family taste in memorials had sobered considerably.' A name, two dates, one short line: 'Steadfast'.

'The real memorial to him was the church bells. The family gave the money to restore those, preferred to spend it that way than on a marble confection. But his funeral was important enough. People came from all over the country for that. The church was quite full.'

They both looked at the sentinel pews. 'Is it ever filled now, at Christmas perhaps?' Rain asked.

'No, not even at Christmas. The last time it was truly full was another Alcombe family service: Sir James's marriage.'

He turned his back on the Alcombe plaque to show her one of Nether Hampton's treasures: a Friendly Society banner. It was a wooden board with pictorial scenes and had been paraded on the society's feast days. With its slender pole it stood perhaps ten feet high and was held to the wall with a spring clip.

They went into the porch, said goodbye, and the rector busied himself at his noticeboards as she walked into a gently falling drizzle.

She was heading for Withy Cottage when there were footsteps behind her in the churchyard and Robin Woodley was with her again.

'You must have been to confess to the murder, and old Hadley wouldn't give you sanctuary?'

'What on earth . . . ?'

'You looked so glum I knew at once it had to be that.'

'I'm not glum. I'm thoughtful. Isn't that what churches are supposed to do to one? What are you doing here, anyway, prowling about among the gravestones?'

65

He held out his palm to the rain. 'The best of excuses. I'm escaping from the castle mud to the bar of the Huntsman. Coming?'

'Not at all, I refuse to queue for it to open. Why don't you come to Withy Cottage instead?'

'I thought you'd never ask.'

She made coffee, and handed him a cup. 'It isn't free, all this hospitality.'

'What then? The washing up?'

'Worse. Information.' She perched on the basket chair.

'Oh no, Rain. Not Adam again, please.' He pulled a face of sham horror.

'Only partly.'

'I knew it . . .'

'Well now, can we get it out of the way?'

'If you must, but I'd rather you let me invite you to dinner.'

'Question one. What did Adam Hollings do before he went away that upset or embarrassed people?'

'Who says he did anything?' It wasn't the question he had anticipated.

'I do, because of the way people react when he's mentioned. I now know *when* he went, which was two months ago, roughly. And I know someone has since broken into this cottage and removed . . . things.'

His surprise looked genuine. 'What sort of things?'

'Letters. As far as I know only letters. Three were delivered in the first week of his absence and put on the desk by Mrs Chidgey. Now there is only one unopened letter there. Therefore . . .'

'Someone has been in and taken them.'

'Exactly. What did Adam do that made him so unpopular? And who would think it worth breaking in here to steal his mail?'

He shook his head, and eventually said, reluctantly: 'Adam could be . . . rather unfeeling sometimes.'

'That's no help. We are all guilty of that. Tell me what he *did*.'

'I don't think there was one grand gesture. All the people whose reactions you have noticed might have different reasons.'

'So what is yours?'

'Have I seemed upset or embarrassed by Adam?'

'You rapidly changed your mind about him. You were here a month before he disappeared and in that time you became friendly with him and then gave it up.'

'I grew wary of Adam. I was being used. That, I suppose, is it: he used people. He wasted my time and I don't have much. You see, the Trust employing me had so many hiccoughs getting the excavation started and the summer had gone by the time I arrived.'

'And summer is the best time because of the weather?'

'And longer days. Well, all through the spring and summer Sir James Alcombe was dithering about when and whether the Trust could have access to the site. He'd agreed last year the work ought to be done. The rector has been leaning on him for years, trying to convince him that the ruin ought to be preserved and studied.'

'Most landowners would be delighted to have that sort of monument on their land, surely?'

'Oh, Sir James is proud of it in his own way, I dare say. He says his reservations are all to do with the effect on Nether Hampton if the castle is tidied up. He's afraid the village would be ruined if it became a tourist attraction.'

'Coaches lined up in the square. Hot dog vans by the church . . .'

'And public toilets in the conservation area. Yes, I think we both see what he has in mind.'

'But your dig is hardly going to threaten Nether Hampton with any of that.'

'Not on its own. Sir James says his fear is that an excavation is the thin end of the wedge. Draw attention to the site by sending in a horde of archaeologists and then everyone will be crying out for the castle to be 'rescued' from leafy obscurity. And then coaches, hot dog vans . . .'

'And public toilets. I see.'

'In the end the Trust got the go-ahead but he let the summer slip away and he imposed so many conditions that I wouldn't have blamed the Trust if it had backed out. The main one was that I must work alone and only outside the curtain wall.'

'As you found the body down a well inside the wall he knows you've broken the rules.'

'He hasn't complained yet. I expect to be summoned to the manor house and banished from the village forthwith. Or strung up by my thumbs in the square, or whatever lords of the manor are allowed to do with miscreants.'

'But how did Adam interfere with your work?' Rain did not know whether Robin was deliberately sliding away from the subject again.

'He said he knew a farmer at Stockway who was very interested in local antiquities, was anxious that a detailed excavation should be made at the castle and knew Sir James Alcombe quite well. Adam told me the farmer, Hugo Brand, could probably talk Sir James into allowing me to have help on the site. More than that, Adam thought it was probable that Hugo Brand would help the Trust by paying for part of the extra help. I had told him the Trust had committed much of its money elsewhere once Sir James had become adamant about allowing only one man on site.'

Rain said that sounded like a good and helpful idea.

Robin nodded. 'That's what I thought at the time. I would have been foolish not to meet this Hugo as Adam suggested and to sound him out. Adam took me to the pub at Stockway, the Flatner, on a Sunday lunchtime when he knew Hugo and his wife and friends would be there. On the way over he cautioned me about not rushing the chap. Well, I should have realized then how tenuous the whole thing was.'

'None of it was true?'

'Not much of it. Hugo Brand is quite keen on what he calls 'my field' and was pleased to have jolly chats with me in the bar. Then he got around to asking me to look at what he thought were some 'interesting things' on his land. I won't burden you with the detail of several visits to the Brand farmlands to cast the professional eye over some pretty unexciting sights . . . And also, of course, Hugo Brand had to come up to the castle and see what I was up to. Several other times.'

'But no help with Sir James, no cash.'

'He knows Sir James slightly less than I do. My hints about helpers and cash withered where they fell. I don't believe there was ever any hope of assistance from him and I don't believe he ever said anything to persuade Adam there was.'

'Adam Hollings made it all up? What reason could he have?'

'Cynthia Brand. That was his reason. I was being used to keep Hugo out of the way for them.'

There was a long pause while Robin remembered the creeping realization of Adam's duplicity and Rain recalled the awkwardness she caused by lobbing Adam's name into conversation with Hugo and Cynthia and their horsey friend Caroline at the Flatner.

Rain told Robin: 'Hugo must have found out about them.'

'Adam told him. He would have enjoyed telling him. You see Adam used to complain that the villages around here don't accept incomers easily, that the social set-up is feudal and the whole rotten system is perpetuated by the Hugo Brands.'

'And yet he chose to play bridge once a week with the lord of the manor!'

Robin laughed. 'Not for the pleasure of Sir James's conversation, he didn't. He had nothing to say in favour of him. But he seemed to have reached a truce with the General and Mrs Corning, and he is actually on very good terms with Joan Murray. Those three are all incomers. One has to admit Adam is right about that. The incomers will always be the outsiders. Joan Murray is probably his only friend in Nether Hampton.'

'An unlikely liaison, surely? They can't have much in common.'

'Perhaps they find each other useful. Anyway, country life is made up of unlikely liaisons. People have to make friends where they can. You've been to Joan Murray's bridge evening: do you imagine the General and Alcombe would choose to spend an evening together once a week if there were other social options? Or that Joan Murray has much in common with Edwina Corning? Or Sir James?'

CHAPTER 8

The sky darkened and it rained heavily all afternoon. Robin stayed to lunch at Withy Cottage and sat in front of the log fire a long time after.

The subject of Adam and his vanishing trick was, to his relief, dropped. His final comment was that whatever had become of Adam he was alive and well and causing havoc somewhere. Any thought Rain might harbour that he'd been murdered and buried at the castle by an angry husband or anyone else with good reason was fantasy born of working for the gutter press.

'You never know,' Rain said.

Towards the end of the afternoon a very wet policeman, Detective Sergeant Paul Rich, called. He was making routine house-to-house inquiries following the discovery of the body at the castle.

He dripped on the doormat and admired the fire. Soon he was sipping tea beside it. He already knew about both Robin and Rain and their part in the discovery. There was polite talk with Robin about local historical sites and the latest theories about Stonehenge. Then there was a more abrasive discussion with Rain about gossip columns and 'why the papers always get it wrong'.

After that he took out a damp notebook and got down to business. 'As you both know very well,' he began ponderously, 'a body has been found buried at Nether Hampton castle.'

They grunted assent. A log spat sparks on to the rug in front of the fire. Detective Sergeant Paul Rich waited until they had safely died. Then he went on: 'As you may not have heard, it is the body of a woman.'

Robin gave Rain an I-told-you-so glance, which she made a point of appearing to ignore. Another log spat on the hearth rug. Again everyone waited until the sparks had blackened.

Rich, with his gentle West Country burr, was telling them: 'Now it appears that this unfortunate woman came to a violent end . . .'

'Murdered,' said Rain, to speed things along.

'She wouldn't have been buried like that otherwise,' said Robin.

Rich cleared his throat. 'As you say, Miss Morgan, we believe she was murdered. We do not yet know who she was . . .'

'Don't they go by the teeth?' Robin asked.

A flicker of irritation disturbed Detective Sergeant Rich's features. He said: 'They can tell a lot from the teeth, Mr Woodley, but it takes time. Meanwhile we are making inquiries about missing people. Now I realize that neither you nor Miss Morgan have been in Nether Hampton very long, but it is just possible you have heard something about someone who went missing from the village a while back.'

Rain shook her head. 'Sorry, can't help.'

'She's been too busy looking for Adam Hollings,' Robin said lightly. 'He's gone missing, hasn't he, Rain?'

The sergeant waited while Robin teased and Rain defended herself. When he saw they had quite finished he asked a few questions about the absent Adam and wrote their answers down.

'He hasn't been seen,' Rain explained, 'since the night the Stranglers played the Smugglers. At Stockway. He was in the pub that night, 3 September. No one in the village admits to seeing him since.' She noticed her voice was curiously formal. Did police notebooks have this effect on everyone?

'No one you've *asked*, you mean,' corrected Rich quietly. He returned to his question about missing people, but they couldn't supply any so he soon finished his tea and reluctantly headed back into the wetness.

The log fire swirled smoke into the room as the front door was opened for him. He pulled up his raincoat collar and, hovering on the doorstep, glanced back at the fire. 'You don't want to burn that stuff, spits real nasty,' he said. And went out.

When he'd gone and the smoke had diminished, Rain said: 'Fancy making me tell him all that about Adam. He can't have been interested. They are looking for a missing woman.'

'It's my literal mind. He just asked about missing *people*. Besides, if we didn't tell him Adam had run off then someone else was bound to and that could look rather sillier.'

'Policemen always make me feel silly. It's as though they are waiting for me to say the tiniest indiscretion, make the slightest mistake, and a uniformed arm will flash out and grab me.'

'Guilty conscience.'

The phone rang. Oliver. Tactfully, Robin left Withy Cottage for the meagre comfort of his room at the Huntsman.

Oliver was idle in the office, missing Rain. He had fixed a weekend off, the one after next. Rain thought that when they did get together she would wring out of him a lot more information about Adam Hollings than he had thought fit to give her. She would like to know whether Oliver had ever had cause to regret knowing Adam. But perhaps not. Oliver was nobody's victim.

'Solved the murder yet?' Oliver was asking.

'I'm working on it. I've just had the police here asking about missing persons.'

He laughed. 'You didn't report Adam, I hope.'

'He came into the conversation but I doubt if they'll comb the countryside for him.' She wanted to change the subject. 'Look, I'd better speak to Holly about the murder now the police are saying that's what it is. Can you transfer me to her? She can pass it on to the newsdesk. If I speak to them myself, they'll think I'm offering to do some work for them.'

There was a gap while Oliver stood on his chair and peered the length of the newsroom. 'Yes, she's sitting there. Looking terribly solemn. Probably wondering what to fill the column with. Did you see today's?'

'No.'

'Well . . . never mind.'

'Oliver, what was it?'

'Let's say the most exciting thing was the apology to Lord Bromfield for her piece the previous day.'

'Oh no, not that story about his race horse?'

'That one.'

'But I killed that last week. It just didn't stand up.'

'Yeah, I know. But God liked it, so Holly was told she had to run it. She doesn't tear up the commandments like you do.'

Rain remarked tartly that it was a pity the editor didn't put his own name on his follies. Oliver transferred her to Holly.

'Hi!' Holly was happy to hear her. 'Fancy you ringing up on holiday.'

'Now you know the *Daily Post* is with me every waking moment . . .'

Holly said: 'Oh-oh, you've seen today's and you're mad at me.'

'No, I haven't seen it. A word with our circulation boys when I get back, I think. They must have missed the train from Paddington again last night.'

'That makes me feel a shade better, knowing our half-dozen West Country readers have missed today's gem.'

'The Bromfield apology? Oliver just told me.'

'Honestly, I *told* them you'd spiked it before you went. But you know what God's like. Sent them out of the evening conference promising to use it.'

'Publish and be damned.'

'And now I'm sitting here feeling damned.'

'Look, I'm going to take your mind off that. I've got a murder for you.' She gave Holly a couple of paragraphs about the body of a woman being found on Sir James Alcombe's estate. She added a few decorative phrases about Nether Hampton and the castle.

'That's all I can give you now, but you should find something about the Alcombes in the record.'

'Family motto, pedigree, whatnot. OK. Have we ever run a story about them?'

'Not in my time, Holly, but the library might turn something up. Let me know what you get?'

'Sure.'

A drenched Wayne Chidgey sloped across the square as Rain put the phone down. His spiky green hair was pasted flat over his skull, his jacket was dark with water. Rain shivered and put another log on the fire. Soon it would be dark and it had been the sort of day which had never really been light. She felt cheated.

Raindrops were sighing down the wide chimney. There was the sound of rushing water outside the back door. Withy Cottage was leakproof. She ought to enjoy being comfortable beside her fire for the evening. She had brought a modest pile of books and had barely opened them.

She knew she wouldn't this evening, either. The blurred shape of the Huntsman was signalling to her across the cobbles. It appealed much more to spend her evening under its thatch, listening to the villagers talking about skittles and the weather.

The bar was fairly full, surprisingly for a midweek evening. Rain recognized Wayne Chidgey's father, Alf, and also the jolly man who had been at the church gate the day the body was found.

The old man who had tried, on her last visit to the Huntsman, to quiz her about gossip columns succeeded this time. The landlady, Mrs Yeo, in another too-tight frock, was glumly taking orders. The ginger cat was on the bar once again. And at a table close to the fire Detective Sergeant Paul Rich was trying to dry out.

Rain took her drink over to him. He was alone and she thought he might prefer not to be.

'Helping the police with their enquiries, are ye?' the jolly man called over and earned a round of laughter.

Rain asked whether Rich had managed to call on all the houses that day. 'Mostly,' he said, pleased to have someone join him. 'There's a few I'll be back for tomorrow. I'm praying for fine weather.'

He grimaced at a steaming wet trouser leg. 'They talk about wanting the police on foot and on pushbikes instead of in cars but they don't think about weather like this.'

She murmured sympathy. She knew it was pointless to ask what information his inquiries had thrown up, much as curiosity was biting at her. Instead she asked whether Nether Hampton, in good weather, wasn't a pleasant place for door-to-doors, the people were so friendly.

He smiled into his beer. 'Friendly? Well, of course, you haven't been here long, have you?'

'Only a few days, but people have been so kind and interested . . .'

'Well, they'd be interested all right. I'm sure you're right there. But you want to try coming here in a police uniform and see how friendly they are then.'

'So they don't help you?'

'They are polite enough, mostly, and if you put the question just right you will likely get to hear an answer. But they aren't going to go a bit out of their way to give you anything you don't ask for.'

He fingered the wet trouser leg with distaste. 'They don't often feel the need of us, to be honest. They'd sooner sort things out their own way. Now years ago . . .' And he told her something of the long history of Nether Hampton's independent spirit regarding outsiders in general and the police in particular.

'So, what I will ask of you,' he said, lowering his voice and leaning towards her, much as she had seen Edwina

Corning talking to Sir James Alcombe on the bridge evening, 'is this. If you hear anything at all that you think might be of interest to the police, then you pass it on. Because there'll be a lot more said in the bar of the Huntsman and in the shops here than will ever be said to me.'

Rain nodded solemnly. She couldn't imagine she would ever do anything of the sort.

After he finished his beer and left she joined the group at the bar. 'He were after your Wayne today, Alf,' the jolly man said to Mr Chidgey.

'Harassing him, weren't he?' Alf Chidgey agreed. His steely hair still stuck up in an imitation of his son's.

'What were Wayne up to?' a beaky-faced woman asked, sensing the makings of a piece of gossip.

'Nothin', Violet,' Alf Chidgey said flatly. 'He were working on that carnival float, that's all. Detective Sergeant Bloody Rich told him he didn't look right, like, working on it when it were pouring down.'

The jolly man laughed. 'Thought he were stealing from it, did he? Shows how much he knows, don't it? Wayne do work real hard on that float.'

The beaky-faced woman agreed. 'He always do, young Wayne.'

The old man with the interest in gossip columns piped up. ''Tis Thursday, carnival. Well he's got to work on him now, 'tis no good working on him when carnival be over.' He also earned a round of laughter.

The Nether Hampton entry for the carnival was being built under the partial shelter of an old Dutch barn in a field on the edge of the village, the old man explained to Rain. He reminisced about how much better the carnival had been when he was a lad, and how the men of the village had thrown themselves into the work of building the float.

''Tis always the same, Joe, looking back for the best times,' the beaky-faced woman said. 'If you ask me 'tis better now than 'twere then.'

The group broke into a hubbub of agreement and disagreement at that. The beaky-faced Violet's voice rose above it. 'And I'll tell 'ee for why. 'Tis summat for the young uns now. 'Tis better for young Wayne and his friends to be doing it all than standing around watching the men.'

'But 'tis competitive, Violet,' Joe argued back. 'We don't win no trophy for the village with a float made by a bunch of kids.'

Robin Woodley chose that moment to come down to the bar from his room under the eaves. The jolly man told him that Rain wanted to go to the carnival and they had been casting around for an escort for her. 'We'm settled you be the very chap,' he said, and the rest of his nonsense was lost in howls of laughter.

'And we'll all be there to see she don't get stood up,' said old Joe. The Huntsman rang again.

'Don't ee mind, they be terrible old matchmakers,' the beaky-faced Violet said to Rain between sobs of laughter. But nobody minded and the date was made.

CHAPTER 9

Wednesday morning was dry and bright. The westerly wind had swept away all trace of wet Tuesday and the hump of the hills looked close and clear. A good day for a drive.

Rain looked on the back page of the *West Somerset Advertiser* for its address, tucked a notebook into her shoulder bag and threw a precautionary raincoat into her car. She switched on Adam's telephone answering machine and left.

The colour-washed houses, the stumpy church and the blue cobbles had a startling freshness. Wayne Chidgey, carrying a hefty spanner, crossed the square, his hair recovered into a cockscomb of brilliant green. The anxious-looking Jessie was entering the iron gates of Laurel House. Edwina Corning's erect figure was popping into the post office and the plump Mrs Yeo was briskly sweeping leaves from the front steps of the Huntsman.

The *West Somerset Advertiser* had its offices in Portlet, a harbour town at the foot of the Quantocks. Once it had been a thriving place, as coal boats had come in from the distant Welsh coast. The Severn Tunnel had ruined it: it was suddenly easier to transport coal by rail than water. Portlet would never recapture its Victorian vigour.

All its grander buildings dated from that heyday and the *Advertiser* had bought itself one of them. In its front office a young girl, familiar only with the routine of handing over forms for advertisers to write down their chosen wording, had been left in charge.

Rain asked whether she might see the news editor and the girl slipped away through a mahogany swing door. The answer ought to be yes: the paper was at the beginning of its weekly routine, panic would not set in for days.

The man who tagged after the girl as she returned to the counter was an energetic forty, slightly greying and wearing thick-rimmed glasses. He switched on a disarming smile as he caught Rain's eye. 'Good morning. Jack Stevens, the editor. How can I help you?' he asked breezily.

'I'm Rain Morgan . . .'

'From the *Daily Post?*' Not at all what he'd expected. His eyebrows went up and he whipped off his glasses, a contradictory move.

'So I am.'

'Well, well. I thought it was going to be someone whose daughter's wedding picture had gone in upside down.' This was probably not a joke.

The girl giggled and toyed with the advertisement booking forms. She couldn't take her eyes off Rain. Rain said to Jack Stevens: 'I'm hoping to find some information in your back numbers. About the Alcombe family.'

'At Nether Hampton, aren't they? We ought to have something for you, but it's rather on the fringe of our area and . . . to tell the truth we don't get many stories out of Nether Hampton.'

'They don't like talking to strangers?'

'They don't like talking to the press. The only time they are willing to is when they want to tell us we've got something wrong. Which is pretty much like other villages.'

'And they don't give you much help in getting things right in the first place.'

He replaced his glasses, lifted the flap in the counter. 'You'd better come through.'

The editorial department had a cubby hole for the editor and four ill-matched desks pushed together so that staff could squabble over two telephones. Battered paper spikes stood on each desk; a plethora of scrawled messages on scraps of paper balanced on three ancient typewriters; and there was a tattered office diary which might *just* make it to the end of the year without its spine tearing through.

Coils of cigarette ash on desks and floor, ripped moquette typists' chairs, bulbous plastic cups that had been filled with boiling water and now hung about displaying coffee dregs . . . the average small-town newspaper office. It was part of the weekly miracle that journalists could work so hard and so cheerfully in the midst of such squalor. There were days at the smart, modern *Post* when Rain, perversely, hankered for all this.

'Everyone's out,' Jack Stevens said as he tugged at an unyielding grey filing cabinet decorated with ancient and faded IMPORTANT! and URGENT! notices. The cabinet lurched open and proved it was grossly overfilled with tatty brown files. Jack Stevens could barely slide his hand between them to draw one out.

'Looks like everyone on our patch begins with 'A',' he joked. At last he won his prize and carefully carried it to a spare table by a grubby window. 'Mind that cable!' he called in warning and Rain stepped neatly over a telephone cord that straggled from the phone point by the window to the desks.

Stevens brushed over the table top with his hand and laid the file down. He flipped it open at nearly brown cuttings. 'They get paler as you go on,' he said with a grin.

Rain thanked him and bent over the cuttings. The Alcombe file was a fat one, which was puzzling. Surely Sir James and his predecessors hadn't been as newsworthy as all that? The first cutting she picked up was about a plan to tarmac Nether Hampton's cobbled square. She skimmed it and in the final paragraph came upon a quote from Sir Arthur Alcombe, Sir James's father.

Stevens hovered helpfully. Rain flicked through a few more cuttings and found much the same. A village story with the smallest mention of an Alcombe.

Stevens said: 'If it's the family you want you'll have to sift through. Village matters have been filed under the name of Alcombe. The paper once had a forelock-tugging chief reporter who thought that made filing easier. Nobody's ever got around to redoing it. If you want anything on a village you had better know the name of the local bigwigs! Unfortunately for us, nobody here has since that chief reporter retired.'

Rain settled to her task. By the end of the morning she had what she had come for, enough detail to supply Holly now and other colleagues later if the body at the castle turned into a story worthy of the *Post's* news pages. There was no photocopying machine available and so she scribbled notes from the cuttings.

'Sorry I can't offer you lunch,' Stevens said, hovering again, 'but it's my Rotary day.' He was ready to go and understandably loath to leave her alone with his precious files. She said she had everything she wanted and they went out together, Stevens leading the way and talking to her over his shoulder.

'Do you know Sir James Alcombe?' she asked.

'We've met, that's all. At functions. He's one of the hunting types and, of course, he's a good name for people to have on their committees. Sir anything is. But he's not much of a socializer or much of a doer as far as I know.'

The file contained an elaborate account of Sir James's wedding to Eugenie Rice. Subsequent stories referred to her doing her share of fête opening, and there were picture stories showing Sir James and Lady Alcombe at hunt balls, Conservative Association dinners and so on. She looked pretty, and probably younger than Sir James.

Rain said: 'What became of Lady Alcombe? She suddenly stops being mentioned in the cuttings.'

'Ah, the Alcombe scandal,' Jack Stevens said mysteriously as he held the front door open for her. 'I'm going this way.' He pointed firmly to the left.

'I'll walk along with you and you can tell me about the scandal.' They went to the end of the proud Victorian terrace and turned off into an older street of low buildings where thatch still lingered. His pace was much too fast for Rain, who put in the occasional skip to keep up.

'Lady Alcombe was a bit of a puzzle by all accounts. She was younger than Sir James and a lot more . . . er . . . lively. I should explain this is all hearsay, it happened before my time. But apparently it caused a fair bit of surprise when they married because no one could see what she wanted with someone like Sir James.'

'Money? Social position?'

'The title, maybe. But she was a whole lot richer than he ever was. No, she didn't marry him for his money. And then . . . We cross here.'

They did, at the double. 'And then there were the rumours,' he went on. 'First she was supposed to be having an affair with this one. Then with that one. Heaven knows if there was any truth in any of it to begin with. And then she ran off. Left him. About ten years ago. She went off with another man and they live in France.'

'So there was a divorce?'

'Not as far as I know. The story goes that he's just hoping she'll turn up again one day. There are supposed to have been one or two contenders for her title, but alas for them Sir James still has a wife. Here we are.'

They had arrived outside a hotel with the Rotary Club sign on show. Rain repeated her thanks and let Jack Stevens get to his meeting. He ran into the hotel.

For her own lunch she bought a couple of weighty sausage rolls, some fruit and a tin of Coke and drove up to picnic in the hills.

There was a glorious view of the Bristol Channel and distant Wales. Right below her lay Nether Hampton but her binoculars, which picked up deer on the hills and tractors above cliffs, offered no detail of the village. The castle was obscured by a wood, the houses were a mere muddle of roofs, and the church tower a poor thing barely poking over trees.

At the rim of the bay were more roofs and a crisp white building which she identified as Stockway and its pub, the Flatner. 'It's all too benign,' she said aloud, 'to harbour a murderer and to be prey to someone as unpleasant as I believe Adam Hollings to be. *And* to have a loose lady of the manor.'

She opened her notebook and glanced down the scribbled lines. Some of it she would pass on to Holly, including her notes on the sale four years ago of Laurel House to Mrs Joan Murray of York. Laurel House formerly belonged to Sir James Alcombe and the sale was mentioned as a puff piece about the local estate agent because he had got a rather high price at auction for the unmodernized Victorian pile.

After a few lines about Laurel House being built as a dower house by the Alcombes soon after they bought Nether Hampton Hall, the reporter mentioned that the sale followed on a number of other substantial sales by Sir James. Several parcels of land had been sold off from the estate.

'So if Lady Alcombe hadn't scarpered, taking the loot with her, your Sir James wouldn't have had to sell anything and you wouldn't be dragooned into playing bridge with a wealthy widow from York,' Holly summed up when Rain rang her.

'Yes, Eugenie has ruined my life.'

'But I can understand her point of view,' Holly said wistfully. 'The West Country is lovely and all that, but who'd want to be there when they could be running off to France with a lover?'

'Can't think of anyone,' Rain lied. 'Now look, Holly, I'm going to be cheeky and ask you to find out a bit of background on Joan Murray for me.'

'Why?' She sounded suspicious. Rain imagined her great dark eyes made slitty, a finger playing contemplatively with a skinny beaded plait.

'Sheer downright nosiness.' Plus boredom. Plus nothing better to do.

'Well, in that case how can I refuse?'

'Good girl.'

Rain put the phone down, and considered the answering machine. She had switched it on by guess and maybe she had done it wrong because Holly said she had phoned in the morning when Rain was out. The machine hadn't answered her. She had just heard the phone ringing out until she had given up.

Rain pressed likely buttons and switches, but without luck. Then she found the instruction leaflet, with a spare tape, in a drawer of the desk. She tried again and the tape rewound. Now she could play back the messages. She heard Mrs Murray's voice.

'Adam,' Mrs Murray said, 'it's me. I want you to ring me as *soon* as you can. It's *very* important. *Ring* me, don't come over.'

The message ended. There was a pause. Another message began. 'Adam, it's Joan again. I *know* you're there, I can see your light. *Why* won't you ring me? I've told you it's very *important*.'

Another pause, another message. Similar but growing more urgent. She ended angrily: 'All right, you can have *all* the money in advance. But please *go*.'

There were no more messages.

CHAPTER 10

Rain had telephoned Holly immediately after she arrived at Withy Cottage. She had gone straight to the telephone on the desk and dialled the *Post*. Only when she had finished the call and played through the answering-machine tape did she go beyond the living room to the kitchen.

Thoughtfully, she filled a kettle, found a teabag and took the teapot and a mug from a cupboard. The taped messages seemed to confirm that she was right, that Mrs Murray had indeed known that Adam Hollings was going away. So why had Mrs Murray pretended otherwise?

Rain fetched milk from the fridge, noticing there was only a trickle left in the bottle. She would have to buy more. And then, as she turned from the fridge, something drew her attention: a shiny patch on the kitchen floor. It looked wet.

She knelt and touched it. Grubby water stained her fingers. The floor covering was brownish and patterned, the sort chosen because it disguises marks so well. If this damp patch had been anywhere except in line with the window, where it reflected light, she would never have spotted it.

With care she looked over the rest of the floor, feeling here and there with her fingers. Nothing. Just that one damp patch: a roughly triangular shape, the widest part towards the

86

door from the kitchen into the lobby. She was convinced it was a footprint.

Tentatively she pushed open the lobby door. It swung a little way and then juddered to a stop. Something was behind it.

She tried to remember what the lobby contained. A cupboard with an immersion heater in it. The door to the garden. The door to the bathroom. The log basket. The doormat. Nothing to obstruct the kitchen door: none of the other doors could be opened to impede it, and if the log basket had been moved behind it then it would have been shoved back again by the kitchen door.

Rain pushed more firmly and the door yielded enough for her to be able to put her head in the gap and peer round.

She laughed aloud, with relief. Imagination had been threatening her but all she saw on the floor was the back doormat. It was rucked up between the kitchen door and the log basket.

She squeezed through and pulled the stiff rubberized mat away. Her own movement with the kitchen door had caused it to ruck up. It would have lain quite flat until she forced it hard against the basket.

And yet, there was another niggling puzzle. She could not understand how the mat had got into the position to be trapped like that.

Rain had not been out of the back door for two days, not since she had done her washing on Monday and heard the Cornings talking in their garden at Hampton House. The back door was unbolted now, and she could not be sure whether she had left it like that.

Opening it she found a puddle left by yesterday's heavy rain. There was no doubt in her mind that someone had come in through the back door while she was out and had left the same way.

She experimented by standing outside the back door and closing it on the latch. Even when she bent down, with her hand through the gap of the door to draw the doormat as close to it as she could, it was impossible to shut the back door and leave the doormat in its usual position.

Whoever had come into Withy Cottage had been careful to leave everything undisturbed this time, but could do nothing about the telltale doormat or the bolt. But how could anyone have got in if she had bolted the door? And if she had forgotten to bolt it, how would anyone have known?

She considered alternatives. Perhaps it was only the escape route downstairs and the access was somewhere else? She realized how easy it would be to clamber up to the back bedroom window: mount the dustbin by the back door; from there get on to the lobby roof; and then the bedroom window, low in the catslide roof, was to hand.

She dashed upstairs to check but the casement was firmly shut. The handle was in the closed position and the metal bar dropped over the retaining knob. The room looked untouched. No, someone had come in by the back door — the footprint, damp from the puddle, insisted on that.

Downstairs again she shut and bolted the back door, noting that for all its robustness the bolt need hardly be there. The metal loop it slid into had only a tenuous hold on the frame.

She put it to the test. She opened the bathroom window wide, placed a chair under it and climbed over the sill and into the garden. Then she went to the back door, raised the latch with one hand and threw her weight against the door. It gave.

The metal loop lost the only nail that secured the bottom of it and the door flew open with the bolt still pushed across. Rain picked up the nail from the lobby floor.

She went into the garden and looked around. The high wall of Hampton House ran along one side of Withy Cottage garden, a six-foot high fence of larch lap separated her from her neighbours on the other side. It would be possible to scale the Hampton House wall but she couldn't think either Edwina Corning or, for all his fitness, the General would do so. And if anyone else did, the Cornings, who were usually at home, would be sure to see them.

Rain walked the distance of the wooden fence. No one would risk climbing those panels. They were unable to take that sort of weight and treatment. Possibly someone could squeeze between them if they weren't securely fixed to the posts, but she found them all firmly upright.

Or one might wriggle around the end of the fence if it wasn't properly butted to the end walls. She checked. There was no gap where the fence met the end of Withy Cottage's bathroom, and none at the other end where it joined a row of stone-built sheds.

Withy Cottage had three sheds, stretched across the width of the garden and making the end wall of it. The sheds were dilapidated. Paint on their wooden doors was dull and flaking after years of negligence and exposure to weather. Their roofs were tiled but sagging. And, again, the Cornings would easily see anyone climbing over them.

The door of the first shed creaked back, disturbing spiders' webs and revealing Adam Hollings's store of logs, a bag of coal and a chopping block with an axe thrust into it.

More webs ripped when Rain pushed open the door of the middle shed. Inside she found garden furniture: four chairs neatly stacked, a table with a hole in the centre to take a sunshade, and, leaning against the wall, the sunshade.

'Then number three must have the lawnmower and gardening tools,' she reasoned. And stopped, her hand poised by the latch. This time there were no spiders' webs intact. Their wispy remains showed how they had already been torn. This door had been opened recently.

Rain was very reluctant to open it again. Although she felt it was unlikely anyone would be hiding in there now, and on the whole people did not discover anything nasty in the woodshed, her hand would not lift that latch.

After all, there was an unexplained murder in the village. After all, there had been a prowler at Laurel House three days ago. The memory of that prowler and the General's over-reaction to him tipped the scale. Rain began to smile at her own timidity. Her hand went for the latch.

She was right about the lawnmower and the precisely arranged rank of gardening tools. But there was something else she had not been ready for. She stood in the doorway staring at it.

Facing her across the shed was another door. Day was fading, so she could make out its outline but little more. Curious now, not nervous, she opened it and found herself standing on a strip of rough ground.

There was an overgrown track that ran behind the main street, but the rest of the area was an unkempt wasteland of grass and weeds. Hampton House also had a door on to the track, so did other neighbours as far along the row as she could see.

Rain walked a few yards but there was no one in sight and no building overlooking the track. Then the church clock struck the hour, reminding her to be quick if she was to buy milk before the shop closed. She hurried back through the shed and into the cottage, pushed the mat against the back door, snatched up her purse and went out.

Several people were already in the shop making last-minute purchases. Mrs Wall, the middle-aged woman who ran the shop, greeted Rain and so did Mrs Chidgey, who was queueing at the checkout. Rain picked up the last pint of milk and joined her.

'No word from Mr Hollings, then?' Mrs Chidgey asked. It occurred to Rain that with Adam away Mrs Chidgey didn't get any work.

She said: 'Nothing, I'm afraid. I'm glad I've seen you, I wondered whether you would like to do Withy Cottage while I'm staying here?'

Mrs Chidgey agreed without hesitation and said she would be in at ten o'clock sharp next morning and they would 'sort things out then'. Rain was quite sure that however delicate Mrs Chidgey chose to be about discussing her affairs, the whole of Nether Hampton would have a very shrewd idea what she earned from cleaning Withy Cottage.

The woman in front of Mrs Chidgey, an elderly woman with grey hair caught in a bun, was dreamily gazing at a shelf of cake mixes and chocolate buttons, unaware that Mrs Wall was ready to serve her.

'Mrs Wood!' the shopkeeper called.

'Your turn, Mrs Wood,' said Mrs Chidgey, and touched the elderly woman's arm.

Mrs Wood apologized for keeping everyone waiting and was soon served and away. Then Mrs Chidgey let Rain go ahead of her because she had only the milk to pay for. Rain left, feeling slightly ashamed at always appearing in a hurry. Hurry, she reminded herself, was a bad habit.

During the evening she telephoned Oliver and told him she was certain someone had been into the cottage while she was out. His advice was to mend the bolt on the back door and secure the shed door, both of which she already planned as priorities next day.

'The point is I've found out *how* someone can get in here but I'm no nearer finding out *why*. Or *who*. It's maddening. I can't think about anything else.'

'Not even the vanishing Adam?' he teased.

'Surely it must all be to do with Adam? No one would be breaking in here because of me. Besides, I know now that Mrs Murray — you know, the woman who invited me to play bridge — well, Mrs Murray not only knows where and when he went, I think she *sent* him.'

She explained about the telephone messages. Oliver said that all she had to do to get to the bottom of Adam's 'disappearance' as she called it, was to 'lean on Mrs Murray for the answers'.

'You make it sound so simple.'

'Because you make it sound so mysterious.' He cut off her protests by saying he wouldn't be able to come to Nether Hampton for the planned weekend after all.

Afterwards she sat grumpily watching television. She could not concentrate on reading and she would not be bothered with a log fire so she switched on the electric fire instead.

Eating her lonely supper she felt miserable at the prospect of going to bed alone in a house where people felt free to wander in and out at will. She wished she had never come to Nether Hampton on her own.

That night she slept badly, waking at the slightest noise or imagined noise. Once she was so convinced someone was there she sprang out of bed and came noisily downstairs switching on all the lights and hoping to make her intruder flee. There was no sign anyone had been there.

For a while she stayed up, drank tea, tried to read. Then she bullied herself into going back to bed and took up with her, for insurance, the biggest of the Sabatier knives from Adam's kitchen.

The only person she frightened with it was herself when she woke suddenly, very late, and found it lying beside the bed. A banging on the front door roused her. She struggled into her dressing gown. It was ten o'clock and there was Mrs Chidgey.

Mrs Chidgey apologized. Rain apologized.

'No, it's not your fault. I've had a bad night, I don't often oversleep.' She ran a deep bath and lay there while the sounds of vacuuming went on in the distance. It was very comforting to hear someone else legitimately busy in the cottage. She was not a person who liked to live alone.

When she emerged, Mrs Chidgey showed her the post that had come: two letters. One was for Adam and was put on the desk, the other for Rain. Oliver had sent her a cartoon depicting the events of the bridge evening. There was a lanky imperious Edwina Corning, a coquettish Mrs Murray, and Sir James throttling a struggling General Corning. Rain and Peppy trembled from head to foot and a vague figure with a cockscomb hairstyle prowled off over a garden wall.

Rain looked at the postmark. The cartoon had been in the post since Tuesday morning and it was now Thursday.

Mrs Chidgey was dusting the desk. 'Shall I put this letter for Mr Hollings with those others?'

'Others?'

'Those that came just after he'd gone. The ones I told you about.'

Rain said quickly: 'No, just leave it on top. I'll see to it later.' And then she asked whether Mrs Chidgey knew of anyone else who had a key to Withy Cottage. She didn't.

Mrs Chidgey preferred to talk about that evening's carnival. She was pleased Rain was going to see it. 'Most of us'll be there from Nether Hampton. We always stand near the bridge, that's where you can see the most. I should try and get a good spot near the bridge if I were you.'

They dealt with the matter of Mrs Chidgey's pay for cleaning the cottage. It was very simple. Rain would pay her whatever Adam did and would need her one day a week.

The hounds and a few riders came into the square. 'Oh yes, twice a week until the end of the season now,' explained Mrs Chidgey. 'Saturdays and Thursdays they're out. Not always meeting here, mind. I should say it isn't more than once a month usually.'

She came, duster in hand, to the window beside Rain. 'It'll be a good turnout. The first ones are. Later on when the novelty's worn off a bit and the weather's unkind they're lucky to get a good handful some days.'

She gestured with the hand that clutched the duster. 'See, there's Sir James Alcombe. Hardly ever misses, that one. Of course, I don't know he's got much to think about now, all on his own in that great place. Only Mrs Wood.'

She automatically began to dust the window frame, making it difficult for Rain to see out. Rain stepped back. 'Who's Mrs Wood?' she wondered, the name familiar but making no connection.

'You saw her in the shop yesterday . . .'

'Yes, I remember now. She's the housekeeper at the Hall, is she?'

'That's right. Been there ever since Sir James's father's time. So whatever has gone on at the big house Mrs Wood's seen it all.' Mrs Chidgey nodded confirmation at this remark, found an aerosol polish and began to drench the living room.

Rain decided it was a good moment to escape to the fresh air of the square and say good morning to Sir James.

She and Mrs Murray, wearing the purple suit and carrying Peppy again, converged on him at the same time. Good mornings were passed around. Lovely days were exchanged. Sir James was leading his mount, a handsome animal, and the two of them a picture of well-bred country life.

'Are you feeling lucky today, Jimmy?' Mrs Murray asked girlishly. Sir James looked pleased with her attention, with life in general.

'It's a good scenting day. We'll draw Cocker's Wood first. We should put up a fox there.'

He turned to Rain. 'Do you ride?' She shook her head. She would be more of a disgrace on horseback than she was at the bridge table.

'Pity,' he said. 'You could have come out with us one day.'

'Oh I'm sure she'd hate doing anything of the sort,' Mrs Murray ticked him off. 'She's a nice girl, she wouldn't want to be hounding poor foxes to death. Would she, Peppy?'

Peppy ignored her, he was much more impressed with Sir James's horse, which was arching its neck to inspect him. Rain wondered whether this wasn't the first time she'd ever heard 'hounded to death' used correctly.

Sir James snorted a laugh. 'Joan, if you want to be respected in the country you're going to have to revise those townie ideas of yours.'

Mrs Murray grew a little pink. A hand fluttered to her hair. Her rings and gold bangles flashed in the sun. She started to reply but Sir James's attention was seized by a disturbance among the hounds and riders behind him.

He swung back to Mrs Murray. 'Did you see that! Something will have to be done about that fool, Corning.'

Mrs Murray 'oh deared' and Rain craned to see what had happened. General Corning was on his grey mare, causing trouble again. Unfortunately for Sir James and Mrs Murray he was heading, somewhat haphazardly, for them. Sir James repositioned his own mount out of harm's way.

The General didn't dismount. He raised his hat with a flourish to Mrs Murray, continued the gesture to include Rain, and began to tell Sir James how he couldn't get any sense out of the master who seemed to think they ought to head straight for Cocker's Wood.

'Won't get a damned thing there, if you ask me. Same as Saturday. Rushing about all ways, no science. Waste of time.'

'We accounted for two, Frank,' Sir James replied calmly.

Mrs Murray said: 'But they were both after you'd fallen off, Frank. That's what you said happened, wasn't it, Jimmy?'

Jimmy looked as though he hadn't heard her and found something important to do with his horse's girth. The General looked as though he had heard her and his colour rose.

Mrs Murray said: 'Better luck today, Frank, eh?'

The General scowled. He jerked his animal away. It lunged and frightened some onlookers. Sir James looked after it. 'Why doesn't he stick to jogging?' He sounded savage.

Rain very much wanted another opportunity to talk to Mrs Murray about Adam Hollings. She was dithering about inviting her back to Withy Cottage for coffee once the hunt moved off. The snag was Mrs Chidgey. Rain did not know whether she would be safely gone by then.

And then Mrs Murray was saying to Sir James how nice it would be if he were to call in for a glass of sherry around seven o'clock that evening and, as an obvious afterthought, how nice it would be if Rain came too.

Sir James accepted but Rain had the carnival as her excuse. 'Just us then, Jimmy,' said Mrs Murray looking not at all displeased.

Caroline Merridge, the horsey young woman Rain had met at the Flatner at Stockway, sidled up on her horse to say hello. Hugo Brand came, too, but not Cynthia who, they said, didn't care for hunting.

Rain wished them all good luck, which seemed to be the thing to do, although her heart was already with the fox. Then the huntsman raised his horn and the hunt trotted out of the square.

CHAPTER 11

The carnival was the real thing. Rain had suspected people were making too much of it, that there wouldn't be many floats and that those would be overpraised. She was delighted to be so wrong.

The carnival was a dazzling excitement of light and music, comparable with any of the great festivals of the world. A hundred and more elaborate floats paraded through the town, each one a brilliant fantasy. Nothing was skimped, no trifle unconsidered.

With Robin Woodley she found a place near the river bridge in the town centre and an unobstructed view. Familiar Nether Hampton faces bobbed among the crowd of a hundred thousand that lined the route. She was glad that the nonsense among the regulars at the Huntsman had brought her here.

'Look, the Nether Hampton float.'

'There's Wayne Chidgey,' Robin pointed out. And there he was. Wayne Chidgey with his parrot hair and peacock blue sash was leaping about as a Japanese warrior in combat with another of the village lads. He was going to have to keep that action up from the time the float set out until the procession ended four miles on. Failure to do so would cost the float valuable points in the competition, and judges were posted right along the route.

The organizers of some of the other floats were less energetic and had elected to stage tableaux instead. That meant that whereas Wayne was condemned to perpetual motion, they were banned from all but the slightest quiver. Holding a pose for the time and distance was at least as arduous as repetitive action.

'That must have taken them months to make,' Rain said of the Nether Hampton float.

'All year,' Robin replied. 'They'll be stripping this one down as soon as the carnival season is over and they'll be planning next year's. It's never-ending. Even when they're not actually building the floats they have to raise money for them.'

An especially breathtaking float swayed in front of them. Every inch had been covered with tiny paper flowers applied by hand. The farm trailer had been transformed into a giant flower basket, the people on it had become choice blooms. So it went on, for two hours. Then the mass of people surged behind the final float and followed it until they stopped near the town hall to wait for the brief firework display that always ended carnival night.

At last it was over, except for the judges' verdicts which would be posted outside the town hall later that night. The crowds seeped away from the main street with its boarded shops and bursting pubs. For the next weeks the scene would be echoed in other West Country towns as the same floats trundled from one competition to the next.

Rain and Robin went back to Nether Hampton, as soon as traffic allowed. It was after eleven o'clock. Their car headlights picked up a pale owl and scurrying frightened animals. The hills and the bay had receded into darkness, they might never have been. Only the road existed.

Robin drove over the cobbled square. She invited him into Withy Cottage and poured whisky. 'Who did this?' he asked, holding up the cartoon which she had left on the desk. 'It looks like . . . Yes, it *is* an Oliver West.'

'I told him about the crazy scenes at the Laurel House bridge party, and he sent me that. Of course, he's never seen the actual people so there's not much physical likeness.' She handed him a glass.

'So this is the opposition, is it?' he said, accepting.

'He ought to come here with me. He's Adam's cousin.' Funny, she thought, putting it that way round. Distancing Oliver.

Robin was still chuckling at the cartoon. 'That's good of Joan Murray, you must have given an apt description.'

'Just the Sybil Fawlty hairdo, and her flirty way with Sir James. Did you know nothing can come of that? That he's married to a runaway wife?'

'Adam told me. He said Joannie, as he called her, was furious when she found out. According to him, Joannie had plans to become the new lady of the manor.' They both laughed. Mrs Murray was not what one expected of a lady of the manor.

'That would be a body blow to the local establishment Adam resents,' she said.

'On the other hand she does have money and he's permanently short of that. He's had to sell off a lot of property and land.'

'I know, but what I don't understand is what he needs it for. Surely the land he farms makes money?'

'Apparently not as much as it ought to. The story is that his tenant farmers got rather generous terms in his father's day and he hasn't succeeded in varying them. His own land is crippled by underinvestment. There's the house, too, which takes a lot of maintenance. The indulgence is his stable. Keeping a handful of hunters doesn't come cheap.'

'But no one can go on for ever selling off assets. What will he do when there is nothing left?'

'Perhaps he isn't worried about the long term,' Robin suggested. 'He's elderly. His heir is a nephew in Dorset and the twain rarely meet so he probably doesn't care very much what happens after his time. It would have been useful, though, if he had sold the castle instead of farmland or Laurel House. He would have got a good price for it, I'm sure. The county council tried for years to buy it from him.'

'But he was afraid of it becoming a tourist attraction and ruining the village.'

'Yes. He is supposed to have promised the parish council that he will never part with it. They were happy to hear that. He'd frightened them entirely with talk of coachloads of trippers all day and *son et lumière* all evening. Oh yes, and he threw in threats of re-enactments of the siege with period-clad private armies looting and pillaging in the village.'

The living-room shutters were open and as they talked car lights swept the square, telling of homing parties of carnival-goers. Much later than usual the lights in the bar of the Huntsman went out. Laughing figures padded across the cobbles. In several cottages, downstairs lights were still on, the evening's fun extended to the limit as friends gathered at firesides for the last drinks.

Nether Hampton's float had not won anything. No one seriously thought it would. It was the effort that counted. For the evening Wayne Chidgey, who had put in most of that effort, was the local hero. Everyone had a good word for him.

Robin left Withy Cottage very late. By then nearly all the other lights around the square had long been dimmed and street lights were only a memory. Rain told him about her intruder and played him the tape on the answering machine but he could think of no explanation for either.

He did a makeshift repair to the back-door bolt, taking one of four screws that held a spice rack to the kitchen wall and using it in place of the loose nail. Then he went.

Rain was unable to forget the vulnerability of Withy Cottage. She wandered restlessly about the rooms, not feeling at all tired. Then she went out to her car to fetch the local map. She would see what it had to tell her about the track that ran behind the cottage.

As she was turning back to the cottage, map in hand, she heard the scream. It came from across the square, she was sure of that. The only light over there was at Laurel House. She ran towards it.

The iron gate and the front door stood open. Yellow light stained the courtyard beyond the high wall. In the doorway, Jessie trembled.

Rain grabbed her arm: 'Jessie, what's happened?'

The answer was incoherent. Rain pushed past her. In the sitting room she found Mrs Murray. Dead.

Mrs Murray lay stretched face down on the carpet, an arm grasping the leg of her reproduction Chippendale chair. Her clothes were askew and one court shoe had come off.

She was wearing the peacock blue silk dress with the mink trimming at the throat. Over it was a warm winter jacket of fawn cloth. Her clothes were marked with blood. Her hands, and what Rain could glimpse of her face, were streaked with it, and it had left its telltale trail over the carpet. Peppy was whimpering, sniffing the spots on the carpet and fussing over the body.

The perfectly coiffured grey hair was barely disturbed. Its coils and curls were intact. But it had slid forward and to the side and partially obscured Mrs Murray's face. It had, all along, been a wig.

Beyond the body the doors to the enclosed part of the verandah were open. A cold draught came through. Rain went back into the hall where Jessie, white-faced and silent, waited dully. 'Where's the phone?'

Jessie looked blankly at her, then pointed to a room across the hall from the sitting room. Once it had been a library. The former owners' shelves had stayed but there were very few books now. An uninspiring collection of china and glass pieces was dotted about them. There was a leather-topped writing table and on it a telephone. Beside it was an answering machine like Adam Hollings's.

Rain had the idea that Joan Murray and Adam Hollings had gone shopping for them together. It was just the sort of frivolous thought that popped into one's mind when there was a horror to be avoided. She rang the police and told them about the horror.

Jessie came into the library, ushering Peppy before her, and closed the door. 'He won't keep away,' she whispered. She was shaking uncontrollably.

'What happened? Why were you here?' Later, she knew, Jessie would be retelling the story until she doubted every word of it.

'I wasn't here. I'd been to my sister's and then I was walking home when I saw Peppy. I was near our cottage when he ran up. Well, of course, I knew he shouldn't be running about at night so I brought him back. There was a light in the sitting room so I thought she must be up. I rang the doorbell but no answer. I had the key in my handbag so I came in.' She shuddered and began to cry softly.

'Did you see anyone on your way here? Or hear anything?'

Jessie shook her head. She rummaged in her mac pocket for a paper tissue and blew her nose. 'Oh, poor Mrs Murray,' she wailed. 'Who would have wanted to do such a thing?' At the time Rain could think of no one.

Sergeant Willett and the lanky PC Smith arrived first. 'A hobby of yours is it, Miss, finding bodies?' asked Smith with a misplaced shot at humour.

Sergeant Willett gave him a quelling look. He said: 'Nobody's touched anything, I hope?'

Rain said they had stayed in the library until he arrived, nothing had been disturbed at all except, possibly, by Peppy. The chihuahua, curled now on Jessie's lap, opened huge eyes and quivered at the sound of his name.

Detective Sergeant Paul Rich came next, with other detectives who took photographs. Dr Edward Markell, the pathologist, was the last to arrive.

'Have you got all you want?' he said quietly to the man with the camera.

'Yes, thank you, Dr Markell. All yours now.'

Markell knelt beside the sprawled body that had once been Joan Murray. He opened his bag, began his examination of the scene, and scribbled in his notebook. Then he carefully eased the grey wig from the head and passed it to PC Smith.

Smith took it delicately by a fat grey curl and lowered it gently into a plastic bag, a look of utter distaste on his face. When he had finished handling it he blew his nose.

CHAPTER 12

Detective Chief Inspector Malcolm Merrett was tall and lean with fair hair. Seated at the leather-topped table in the Laurel House library he looked comfortably at home, a youngish country gentleman in a good suit and with an air of assurance. But there should have been books on the surrounding shelves, instead of a clutter of ill-chosen china and glass. And there should have been ancient volumes spread on the desk instead of a sheaf of handwritten police statements.

He looked up briefly as Rain came in, waved her to a chair and carried on reading. She watched him deliberately not watching her. He was going through the statement she had made to Sergeant Willett the previous night before the body had been taken away and she and Jessie had been allowed to go home.

He was holding the sheet of paper loosely between long fingers, fair eyelashes flickering as he scanned it again and again. Then he let it flutter on to the desk and the clear blue eyes fixed on her.

'Funny name,' he said. 'Rain.' There was a ghost of a smile, a private smile not a warming friendly one. 'Why Rain?'

She did not match the smile. 'I had trouble spelling Rhian when I was three. It stuck.'

The smile grew. A finger prodded the statement. 'You say you heard a scream and ran over here . . .'

'Yes, it was Jessie screaming. I found her in the doorway when I arrived.' He knew all this, it was in the statement.

'The front door?'

'Yes, but the door from the covered verandah to the garden was open, too.'

'You went through there? Did Jessie go through there?'

'No, neither of us, only as far as the sitting room.'

'So how . . . ?'

'I could feel the cold draught in the sitting room.'

He nodded, took up a fountain pen and made notes on a ruled pad. Then: 'You also say you were home not long after eleven. Your cottage — I mean the one you are borrowing — looks across the square towards Laurel House. Did you see anyone come to the house?'

'No one. The shutters were open and I was in the sitting room . . .'

'With Mr Woodley.'

If he knew all this why was he asking her? 'Yes. I was facing the window. There was quite a lot of activity earlier in the evening, people leaving the pub and so on, but I didn't notice anyone in the square for a long time before I heard Jessie scream.'

He said matter-of-factly: 'And people were leaving the Huntsman until nearly midnight.'

She hesitated. He said: 'We all know about carnival night. Shall we assume you didn't time them but they probably left the pub not later than midnight?'

She agreed. What was it she'd said to Robin? 'Policemen always make me feel silly. It's as though they are waiting for me to say the tiniest indiscretion.' Chief Inspector Merrett was doing it to her now, and he knew it. He made some more notes, then looked up under fair lashes.

'The street lights were working?'

'Oh yes, the square was well lit until they went out about 11.30.'

'And then it was in darkness out there and yet you say you saw people leaving the pub half an hour later? A dark night as I recall, no moon.'

'I . . . The light from the pub itself showed some figures walking away from it. And then there were torches. People had torches.'

'So you wouldn't have seen who the people were, just the torches moving over the square.'

'That's right, but I didn't notice anyone — or any *torch-light* — going towards Laurel House.'

He leaned back in the imitation-leather club chair and his eyes wandered the topmost shelves where twirly glass vases told of Spanish holidays.

'Not even Jessie's torch?' he asked softly.

There was a long pause before she quietly answered: 'No.'

He carried on scanning the shelves. When he spoke again it was in the same soft tone. 'But Jessie was carrying a quite powerful torch. You must have noticed that when you left here together last night?'

Her yes was barely audible. She knew now what was coming.

He said: 'In your statement you said you were sure no one had come to Laurel House.' He straightened in the chair and slowly pushed the paper over the leather top towards her. 'You're not at all sure, are you?' His voice had taken on a sarcastic edge.

Rain felt her face colouring. She snapped back at him: 'That was written in the early hours of the morning. I'd had a shock, I was very tired . . .'

'And you'd been to the carnival.'

'I wasn't drunk, if that's what you are suggesting.'

'And you weren't exactly poised at your window with binoculars trained on Laurel House!'

'I was with a friend, talking.'

'Just talking.'

'*Talking.*'

'And he is actually the last person you know of who walked towards Laurel House before you heard the scream.'

'The Huntsman is vaguely in the same direction as Laurel House as one leaves Withy Cottage.' She tried for patience, but sounded petulant.

There was a long silence which neither of them would break. Eventually Merrett took up his fountain pen and made some more notes. After that, he said he thought she had better amend the original statement because it had sounded misleadingly positive about what might or might not have gone on in the square. Suppressing her anger she did so.

Back at Withy Cottage she crossly made a sandwich lunch, savaging the loaf and attacking the butter as though that would succeed in distressing Detective Chief Inspector Merrett. Then there was a tap on the front door and Robin Woodley was there to commiserate.

'What's he up to?' he wondered when they had swapped interview experiences. 'I was practically accused of being the murderer because I was the last known person to be crossing the square. Apparently they've only got your word and mine for that, no one else saw me and Mrs Yeo doesn't know what time I slipped into the Huntsman.'

'I felt I was being accused of attempting to mislead the police.'

He helped himself to a sandwich. 'In the Huntsman they're saying Jessie left Laurel House in tears this morning, he had given her such a grilling.'

'And Detective Sergeant Rich can't understand why people here don't fall over themselves to help the police!' She bit into a sandwich. 'Who does the public bar of the Huntsman find guilty?'

'I think *they* are going to wait for a bit of evidence before fingering anyone.'

Holly telephoned from the *Post* with the news that she had found out some information about Joan Murray. 'Sure I got it. Just checked the Murrays who'd died in or around

York five years ago and found the one who'd left a widow called Joan. Got your notebook at the ready?'

While tea was being poured Frank Corning seized the knife and cut himself a broad wedge from a cream sponge. His wife saw and pretended not to. She helped Rain to a daintier slice and herself to another.

'Well, come on, then,' said the General, suddenly cutting across the women's talk. He was using his jollying, hearty tone. 'Tell us all about it!'

'Frank . . .' Edwina admonished.

'Finding Mrs Murray?' Rain asked, without need.

Frank Corning spoke through a mouthful of sponge cake. 'Mmmmm . . . What do you know about it all?'

Rain swiftly ran through the scream, the frightened Jessie, the bloodstained figure in the sitting room and the arrival of the police. There was nothing the Cornings would not have heard from other sources by now.

'What time was all this? Pretty late, wasn't it?' The last of his sponge cake disappeared into his mouth. A blob of cream clung to his moustache.

'Nearer one than anything else,' Rain replied. 'You didn't hear anything yourselves?'

The General shook his head. Edwina said: 'We were asleep by then. Oh, we'd heard people coming back from the carnival earlier, but nothing as late as one.'

'Battered, was she?' the General asked spooning sugar into his tea.

'I can hardly say. She was collapsed in the sitting room and there was blood.' She remembered the dislodged wig. It seemed gratuitously unkind to mention it.

'They were saying in the shop that it was head injuries,' Edwina Corning reported. 'Poor Joan. She didn't have much luck.' She sighed.

Her husband scoffed. 'No good feeling sorry for her now. You weren't too pally when she was alive.'

'Frank! That's most unfair.' Edwina's throat reddened. She turned to Rain: 'You mustn't listen to a word of it. That's just Frank's nonsense.'

Frank Corning laughed loudly, pleased at what he had achieved. 'No good getting in a tizzy. I'll give you a decent alibi. But the fact is, you were always bitching about her. Didn't think she was half good enough for your friend, Sir James, did you?'

Edwina Corning's mouth tightened. She adopted her superior air. 'All this means,' she explained to Rain, 'is that I thought she was embarrassingly obvious in her pursuit of Jimmy Alcombe. I expect you noticed that yourself.'

Rain got as far as a doubtful: 'Well . . .' when Frank Corning broke in: 'Put your nose out of joint there, old girl. Always been chums, haven't you? You and Jimmy Alcombe.'

Edwina said: 'Frank, that sort of remark could be seriously misinterpreted.'

'Not by me,' Rain said, laughing it away. She switched the conversation to family photographs on the mantelpiece.

'Yes, we have two daughters,' Edwina Corning said eagerly. She handed one of the photographs to Rain. 'Susannah and Natasha. Old photographs, of course. They're well grown up now.'

'Get their looks from their mother,' said Frank Corning with pride. They had their mother's fine features and erect posture.

Edwina took the photograph back and passed another to Rain. 'Here they are again.' And so they were, even younger, playing on a sloping lawn amidst a group of adults.

'Recognize that, do you?' Frank asked. 'Laurel House,' he went on, not giving Rain a chance. 'When the Barkers rented it, years before Jimmy sold it to Joan Murray.'

'Oh yes, I can see the verandah in the background now. What was the gathering? A party?'

He said the Barkers had opened the gardens to raise money for the carnival float. Rain pictured the rather featureless expanse of the Laurel House garden, its sloping lawn with just a flower border below the verandah.

The answer was immediate. Edwina said: 'They were very keen gardeners. That garden used to be a delight. Joan Murray wasn't interested and had everything ripped out and made over to lawn, except the kitchen garden. That is still there.'

'Bitching again,' said her husband. She ignored him. He leaned across to Rain and jabbed a finger at the photograph. 'Can you guess who that is?'

Rain could. She said nothing. He told her. 'That's Eugenie, Jimmy's wife. Now, then. Bet you didn't know he had one.'

'Where is she now?'

He gave an elaborate shrug. 'Done a bunk.'

'She is in France,' Edwina said with less drama. She collected the photograph from Rain and replaced it on the marble shelf. 'It's not so mysterious. She went off with a man and they live in France. Jimmy is in touch with her.'

'I see,' said Rain, who didn't.

'Pity she's not in touch with you, Edwina,' Frank said. 'Downright bad manners, if you ask me.'

His wife gave him a look which pointed out that she had not. He said to Rain: 'Edwina has known her since they were girls. Introduced her to Jimmy Alcombe. Helped her out of scrapes.'

'Frank!' Edwina said.

'And then she does a bunk and not a word!' He passed his cup up for a refill. As Edwina poured, he eyed the gap between his chair and the tray with the sponge cake on it. She had positioned it just too far away for him to reach without clumsy effort. He knew she knew that.

'People have their reasons,' Edwina said, to show she wasn't hurt at her friend's neglect.

'Damned if I know what hers could be. You were pretty good to Eugenie. Mind you,' he said to Rain, 'can't say I'm surprised. They were ill-matched if ever a couple were. Old

Jimmy's really only bothered about hunting, and she wasn't one for the country life. Didn't settle, if you know what I mean.'

His face jerked into a wink. Rain knew quite clearly what he meant. Edwina saw too. She said: 'Let's just say it didn't work out for them.'

Rain was finding it difficult not to stare at the cream on the General's moustache. It waggled at her each time he spoke. He said: 'People can't see why Jimmy hasn't divorced her.'

'Perhaps he still hopes she will be back?' suggested Edwina.

'Bringing the funds,' said Frank bluntly. 'That's where the money is, you know, Rain. He's bust.'

'Not quite, Frank,' Edwina said with quiet patience. She felt the weight of the teapot, hesitated, then said she must make a fresh pot.

She could hardly have been through the door before Frank Corning was leaning across to Rain and telling her in a low voice: 'Edwina knows a lot more about all this than she's prepared to say. Jimmy confides in her, you know. She sees the letters he gets from France. Oh, maybe once or twice a year.'

He shot a furtive glance at the closed door. 'Came as a shock to Joan Murray that he'd got a wife and she wasn't going to be lady of the manor. So she was asking what everyone else was asking: why doesn't Jimmy get a divorce? Well now, Jimmy's been asking Eugenie and she's been turning it down.'

'Can't he just go ahead and divorce her?'

'Ah yes, but there's the money. I'm not privy to the arrangements but divorcing Eugenie would be like killing the golden goose. The Alcombe lawyers were quite clever. They made sure the estate would benefit from her money. She has to sign papers to release it and Edwina says she's being a bit naughty and won't do it.'

The cream on his moustache was bobbing excitedly. Rain made an effort not to giggle. She did not know what to say and wished for Edwina and the teapot.

The General slid even further forward on his chair so that he was precariously balanced on the edge. His face was disconcertingly close to Rain's. 'Don't you believe half of the bad news you'll hear about Eugenie. She was a lively lass and a likeable one. It's a pity she's being sticky about the money for the Alcombe estate, and a pity she's snubbed Edwina since she's been away, but there's a lot to be said in her favour, all the same.'

Rain hoped to be told what that was, but the General overbalanced and recovered himself on all fours on the hearth rug. When he was safely back in the chair Rain asked: 'Did you all know the man she went off with?'

The General wiped a hand across his moustache, discovered the cream and licked his finger. 'No, we never heard a word about him until she went off. Jimmy knows, of course. Now that's what I mean about Eugenie: there was often talk and she mightn't always have been too careful, but when it was something serious enough to run away for . . . Well, no one had an inkling.'

They considered silently for a moment. Then he said: 'I mean only Jimmy knew. She told him, and told him she was going. None of her friends knew. Not one of us.' He looked a little sad.

Edwina Corning came back with the teapot and looked round unconcerned, suggesting to Rain that she was quite anxious about what dangerous nonsense Frank might have been passing on.

CHAPTER 13

It was barely light when they set out for York. 'To think I'm doing this for pleasure. I must be mad,' Robin groaned. He reclined the car seat and pretended to sleep. 'Wake me up in Yorkshire.'

'You'll miss the best of the day.' She let the little red car rumble over the cobbles and then down the dip to the church and away.

'Good.'

'Well, as long as you don't snore.'

He yawned. 'I hope you didn't bring me for scintillating company. I don't scintillate until quite late in the morning.'

'I brought you because I might need a witness.'

'Good God, what are you planning? An accident? Or a bank raid?'

'Just to talk to some people. It will be handy to have someone to corroborate what they say.'

'And what *are* they going to say?'

'I've no idea. I haven't asked them yet.'

He groaned again and shut his eyes. 'I'm much better at digging holes in the ground.'

By the time she was watching the bay emerge from the night, Robin Woodley was asleep.

It was true, what she had told him, so far as it went. But she had wanted company, too.

She waited for a set of traffic lights on the fringe of the town to change and looked down at the calmly sleeping figure beside her. A light dusting of freckles. Long reddish eyelashes.

People never saw themselves, only posing, reversed in a reflection. They never knew how they looked when the mind was at rest and the face an unthoughtful blank.

The lights changed. It had been an unnecessary halt, the car had the Saturday streets to itself. Moments later she was through the town and speeding on to the motorway. A couple of lorries trundled a long way ahead, otherwise it was empty. Robin stirred but did not wake as the car swung over to pass them.

If it had been Oliver beside her he would have never relaxed for a second. They would probably have set off arguing about the arrangements. Were they allowing enough time or too much? Were they choosing the right route? Wouldn't it be better to hire a more powerful car?

Also, he would have wanted to drive most of the way, impatiently cursing other drivers and lane-hopping to the exasperation of Rain and everyone else on the road. Yet it would all be turned into a marvellous running joke that made life with Oliver such hectic fun. Occasionally, when the jokes fell flat, there was misery and then she left.

Twice she had left. She had gone back at his insistence that they both knew they could not do without each other. She believed they both knew that was untrue, but they had got together again anyway. Besides, it *was* awkward for her to leave. It was her flat.

Rain made herself stop thinking about Oliver and concentrate on the day ahead. Holly Chase had given her the business address of Sabild, Joan Murray's late husband's business, and also the address where he lived at the time he died. She meant to visit both those places to begin with.

'Why?' Robin demanded over breakfast in a motorway café. They had both opted for toast and coffee, because nothing much could go wrong with them.

113

'To find out what sort of state the business is in now, and why. I want to know what kind of lifestyle Joan Murray afforded before she retired to Nether Hampton. And, yes, I expect the main reason is that I'm a nosey busybody.'

He offered the final piece of toast. She waved it away and he spread the scrapings of a diminutive plastic pot of marmalade on it. 'They'll recognize you, won't they? Doesn't that matter?'

She shrugged. 'I don't know yet. Anyway, they won't recognize you.'

Robin paused with the toast half-way to his mouth. 'Oh no!' he protested. 'I'm here in case you need a witness, remember?'

She sprang from the table. 'No time to argue about that now. I feel the call of the open road.'

He was still eating the toast as they crossed the car park.

The road grew steadily less open, but they made York in good time. 'Where now?' Robin asked as they crawled past the city boundary in heavy Saturday-shopper traffic.

'Any likely-looking tourist office or stationer's where I can buy a city map.'

The stationer's came first, and along with the map Robin bought the local papers. Rain scanned them but there was not a line in them about Joan Murray's murder. Pleased, she tossed the papers into the back of the car.

Next she looked for a public telephone. She had with her the slim black box whose signal over a telephone line allowed her to check whether there were any new messages on Adam Hollings's answering machine.

It was curious to hear her own voice answer when she dialled Withy Cottage. Using the spare tape from the desk she had recorded a fresh message. A high-pitched tone from the remote control and she was listening to a message from Oliver, saying only that he had called. He had neglected to do so the previous day.

The Sabild offices were in a run-down part of the city. The nameboard, white letters on a green background, was faded and peeling but easily noticed as the car turned into the narrow approach road. In the wall beside it were double gates leading into a yard.

Rust was devouring a lorry parked inside and the area was littered with the debris of the trade. Across the yard was a door into the flank wall of an adjacent building. Rain led the way through the sand and mud to it.

No name was displayed but the door opened at her touch and she was standing in the Sabild office. A young woman at a typewriter looked up, stared in surprise at Rain and asked whether she could help.

'I'm looking for a company called Branscombes. I thought this was the address but I must be wrong. Do you know where they are?'

The young woman shook her head slowly, considering. No, she knew of no company of that name.

'They can't have been here before Sabild, perhaps?' Rain persisted, looking puzzled.

'Oh no. Sabild's always been here ever since it began, that's going back to the fifties.'

'I see.' Rain appeared doubtful. 'Sabild didn't have other premises and sublet this place?'

The young woman frowned. 'I've never heard of anyone else having this yard . . .' She brightened. 'But Sabild did have the offices on the other side of the yard once. Actually, they built them.'

She took a little pride in that, and then, with a glance over the cramped and untidy room, she added by way of explanation: 'That was in Mr Murray's time. It was Mr Browning who sold that off and moved the office in here. He runs the business now, you see.'

Rain nodded, prompting her. 'Is Mr Browning building office blocks, too?'

'No, nor houses. They used to do a lot of houses. It's all the small stuff now. Extensions. Conversions. Sometimes we get a . . . But I'm not being much help if you're looking for . . . What was it called?'

'Er . . . Branscombes.'

'Yes, Branscombes.' She frowned again, concentrating on the unfamiliar name. 'Sorry, I can't help on that one.'

'Never mind, thank you for trying. I'm sorry I've interrupted your work.'

'Oh, I don't mind.' The woman laughed. 'Actually, it's the only thing that's happened today. I don't know why I trouble coming in on Saturday mornings.'

When they had picked their way over the yard Robin asked in a loud whisper: 'Who are Branscombes?'

'No idea, I just had to think of a name.'

'But that poor woman is going to go around all week asking people if they remember Branscombes.'

'Don't fret, I've done her a favour. She obviously hasn't got anything else to do.'

'Except her typing.'

'She had a novel beside the machine. Unless she uses it to practise copy typing I should say she just sits there reading.'

'There was paper in her typewriter. I saw it.'

'First rule of office life. If you are going to sit and read a book make sure you have got paper in the typewriter so you can look busy. Anyway, did you hear any typing before we went in?'

He hadn't. Back in the car Rain pulled a notebook out of her pocket. 'I'm noting everything she told us about Sabild, and all the things that struck me about the place.'

'Like the novel beside the typewriter?' he asked ironically.

'That's not mirthmaking. I'm more interested in that lorry as a guide to the health of the company.'

'Lots of builders' yards have an old wreck rotting quietly away.'

'Yes, but Sabild — or what is left of Sidney Murray's business — is reduced to using that one. When it gets smashed they don't spend money repairing it and so the rust is chewing it up. But it's got a current excise licence and it's been used recently.'

'Don't tell me, Sherlock,' he mocked. 'You felt the bonnet and it was still warm.'

'No, I looked at the windscreen. Despite the filth all over the lorry the windscreen and the wing mirrors were clean.'

Rain was skimming through the street names listed on the city map. Berrow Close was on the very edge of the city, a protrusion into farmland beyond. She started up the car.

'I wonder,' Robin said, 'whether you'd mind telling me what the ruse is going to be this time?' They were nearing the close. 'Unless you want me to pose as your deaf and dumb cousin, I think you had better give me a clue.'

'Don't panic, this will be very straightforward. All I want is a good look at the place. I might not even have to get out of the car if it's one of those all-revealing modern boxes.'

But Berrow Close was not like that. There were only eight houses, arranged around a lawn broken by mature trees whose survival had no doubt been a requirement of the planning permission to develop the site. The trees were not only decorative but provided added privacy for houses which were already very private. On one there was a For Sale sign.

The plots were vast by modern standards and each house crouched behind screening shrubs. Number 4 was barely visible through a rose-hung pergola.

'This doesn't reveal anything at all,' said Robin.

'That's why I'm going in.'

'And you would like me to come.' Resignation.

'Just in case I get savaged by alsatians. You never know when another scream will be handy.'

His face told her he hadn't even imagined unkind dogs. They drove cautiously up the drive, stopped outside a bank of garages and went through the pergola to the front door.

'What will you say?' he whispered.

'Don't whisper. It looks suspicious,' she whispered back.

A woman in her late forties came to the door. She was fashionably dressed in casual clothes, a welcoming smile on her carefully made-up face. Rain explained she was trying to contact Mrs Murray who used to live at that house and wondered whether the woman had a forwarding address.

'Yes, I'm sure I have it somewhere. Or my husband has. He's the methodical one in our family, but he's out playing golf. Won't you come in while I find it?'

Rain got Robin an invitation too. They followed in the woman's wake across a spacious hall that ran down a few shallow steps into a sitting room. On a first impression it rivalled Wembley Stadium for size. The second impression was that it contained two of the biggest Dobermann pinschers the world had ever seen.

The dogs were standing alert, poised for action. The woman said: 'OK, Bill and Ben. Sit.' The dogs sat but kept their eyes on the visitors.

Rain realized she and Robin were standing nervously close in the acreage of the room. She took a few casual steps away, prepared to remark on the view from the floor-length windows.

Bill, or maybe it was Ben, was on his feet immediately. Their owner had her back to the dogs. Rain stopped moving. It was safer.

'I'm sure I won't be a moment,' the woman murmured, riffling through the drawers of a desk.

In reply Rain mentioned the magnificent view. The end and one side of the room were entirely glass and gazed for miles over open land. While the rustling of the papers went on the three of them discussed the merits of the view and the dogs waited their chance.

Then Rain unzipped her bag to find a handkerchief, sneezed, and Bill and Ben were in front of her in an instant. Their owner shrieked at them: 'It's OK, Bill and Ben. I've told you once. Now be good dogs and *sit.*' She had only to tell them another three times and they did so.

Rain and Robin exchanged weak smiles. Rain prayed she would not need to sneeze again. The woman apologized: 'I'm not a doggy person myself, I must confess. But living in a place like this one has to be so careful . . .'

Rain and Robin disgusted themselves by sympathizing. The woman held out to Rain a torn page from a telephone pad. 'This is the address we were given. Of course, it was a few years ago. She may not be there now.'

Rain anticipated the familiar address: Laurel House, The Square, Nether Hampton, Somerset. She took the paper from the woman.

'I'll copy it down, if I may.' She unzipped her shoulder bag again, felt for the notebook and pen. The woman was smiling in her friendly way, unconcerned that her own helpful welcome was outweighed by the attentions of Bill and Ben.

Rain wrote quickly, and zipped her bag up again. Relief at being free to leave made her emphatic in her thanks.

'No trouble at all,' the woman said. 'It was nice to have visitors. I don't get too many callers, tucked away up here.'

'Ah, but you've got Bill and Ben for company,' Rain said ambiguously.

Robin waited until they were in the car and moving back down the drive before giving one of his groans. 'I wouldn't mind if she had been going to tell you something you didn't know. But having to stand there terrified for fifteen minutes while she looked up Laurel House, Nether Hampton . . . And then you prolonged the agony by keeping us there while you wrote it down!'

Rain thrust the notebook at him. Silently he stared at the address she had copied down. It was 14 Markland Avenue, York.

CHAPTER 14

Rain stopped the car on the road outside the close and took up the city map again.

Robin said: 'What's gone wrong, then? Are we chasing the wrong Mrs Murray? Was the one at Nether Hampton different from the one married to Sid the Builder?'

'That bit we've got right. That's what Holly Chase found out for me. It's in the record when he died, what his business was, where it was and his home address when he died. We also know he left a widow, Joan.'

'And left her very rich.'

'Rich enough to buy Laurel House but not nearly as rich as builders' widows can be. I'm just going by the will. For all I know there could have been a lot of money already in her name.'

'Even if she was only left the Berrow Close house she'd have had a lot of change when she cashed it in and moved to Nether Hampton.'

'Yes, and after paying for that lavish kitchen and all the other expenditure on Laurel House she would be left with a very good pension. I can't think why Markland Avenue comes into it. Look.' She pushed the map across to him. 'Fancy selling a Berrow Close property and moving to a district like this? Even as a stopgap on the way to Nether Hampton it wouldn't make sense.'

Robin folded the map. 'Suppose we unravel this over a pub lunch? If I don't eat something soon I shall die of lack of nourishment and then you will have to explain that away too.'

'Fine, but somewhere boring. There are too many visual distractions in York and I don't want to waste time.'

'You must be hell to work with,' Robin said amiably.

Not far from Markland Avenue they pulled into the car park of a corner pub that relied on local trade in the evenings and factory workers most lunchtimes. The Saturday menu was scant.

Rain ordered a beef sandwich, Robin a pork pie. The landlord offered peas with the pie and Robin asked for chips, too. He was assured they only did peas.

When the pie came he saw why. It was hot and floated in a dish of grey-green mushy peas. Mint sauce was poured liberally over it.

'I don't believe this!' Robin whispered.

'Don't whisper, it looks suspicious,' Rain once more whispered back.

'I *am* suspicious. If there was anything to be suspicious about, this pork pie is it. Why have they done this to me?'

'I imagine it's a test to discover whether you are as hungry as you claimed you were.' She cut through the doorstep of her beef sandwich, giggling.

'Don't laugh too soon, you might find they've slipped the Yorkshire pudding in along with the beef.'

After much doubt and sorrow he ate the pork pie, most of the peas and declared it a culinary experience that no one should miss. It ought, he insisted, to make the cookery column of the *Daily Post*.

'I have heard tell,' Rain said, 'that hot pork pies are sometimes served with a garnish of black pudding.'

He wouldn't believe a word of it, and although she argued it must be true and cited the cousin of a colleague's friend who had once brought the subject up in conversation in Chelsea, he was unconvinced. She accused him of regional prejudice and they resumed their drive to Markland Avenue.

'Do you mind if we throw our hats in first this time?' he asked as the car straddled a yellow line.

'Don't be silly. This house is not too big for a budgie with agoraphobia.'

It was a 1930s semi-detached house with pebbledash front and the minimum of mock-Tudor influence on the gable above the bay window. The bell was broken and the noise of the knocker inaudible in the street because of the volume of traffic. Number 14 Markland Avenue was not a desirable residence in anybody's language except, possibly, an estate agent's.

The woman who came to the door was rounded, motherly and had faded golden hair that would shortly be white. Rain explained she was looking for a Mrs Murray.

'I'm Mrs Murray. How can I help you?' Polite but not confidently welcoming as the woman at Berrow Close had been.

A lorry roared by and Rain waited until it was possible for them to hear each other before she spoke again. 'I wonder whether we could talk for a few minutes. I'm a journalist doing some research and I think you might be able to help me.' Another truck drowned out the rest of her story. She didn't repeat it.

The woman said, undecided: 'You're sure you're not selling anything? Or collecting?'

'Definitely not. Here.' Rain whisked her press card out of her bag, tried to whisk it back before it could be read. Mrs Murray had hold of the edge of it.

'Oh, Rain Morgan. Oh, is it really you? I thought you reminded me of somebody . . . I always read the *Post*.' Another lorry. 'Come in. And your friend, is he coming too?'

'If you wouldn't mind, Mrs Murray.'

They all trooped down a short cramped hall and into a quiet back sitting room where a three-piece suite left them barely enough room to move. Mrs Murray said: 'We'll have some tea, shall we?'

When she returned, she chose a chair with her back to a strip of garden, settled herself and said: 'Well, now. What is it you'd like to know, dear?' Her reserve had gone, she was curious. It wasn't every day she was interviewed by a famous newspaper columnist.

Rain plunged in. If she had had to do it on the doorstep it would have been riskier but when someone has taken you into her home, made you a cup of tea and called you 'dear', you are fairly safe. You are unlikely to be thrown out on the pavement until you have been allowed to drink your tea, whatever happens. Rain was prepared to make the tea last a long time.

'I'd like to know about Sabild, how your late husband built it up and what has happened to it since.' It didn't matter what Rain said about it, the name was the trigger.

Mrs Murray gave her a long straight look, glanced at Robin who was struggling to appear part of the proceedings without being called on to take part. Mrs Murray said accusingly: 'Who sent you to see me?'

Rain said: 'I went to Berrow Close. The people there had a forwarding address.'

Mrs Murray got up heavily from her armchair, turned to look down the strip of garden and sighed. She said: 'Who else have you asked about Sabild?'

'No one. You are the first.' Tell me, she thought, let me have your version first.

Another sigh. 'There's a lot I could tell you about Sabild, but there's not a lot I'd like to see in the papers. Do you follow me?'

'Of course. All I want is background information. Anything you could tell me would be very helpful.' People always wanted to help. They fell over themselves to appear knowledgeable and useful.

Mrs Murray turned to face Rain again. She nodded firmly. 'All right. I've decided to tell you because it's clear you've got off on the wrong foot and if anyone can put you right, I can.'

Rain waited. Mrs Murray sank down into her chair. 'First off, I've got to tell you that Sid Murray was not my husband.'

Robin said: 'Oh?' and both women looked briefly at him. Rain said: 'So you and he . . .'

'We lived together. I changed my name to Janice Murray and we let people assume we were married. We would have married but it was never going to be possible. You can guess why. The Murrays were Irish Catholics and there was already a Mrs Murray. Joan, she was called.'

She broke off and drank her tea. Rain feared she might be reconsidering, now that she had straightened out that muddle, whether to give anything else away.

Rain said: 'And so you and Mr Murray lived at Berrow Close?'

'That's right. We were together for six years and most of that at Berrow Close. *She* — Joan, that is — was never there. He bought it for me, he said. Used to call it my pension. Well, he knew he had heart trouble, and he was a good bit older than me.'

Rain was puzzled. Holly had definitely referred to a will. What Janice Murray was saying did not tally with that. 'And yet . . .'

'And yet he died and the lawyer came to me and said: 'It's bad news again, Janice, Berrow Close is hers.' Well, I passed out. I mean, I really collapsed.'

Over the next hour Rain got the detailed Janice Murray version of events. The main threads were the ambitious and manipulative Joan Murray who pushed her husband way beyond what he might have achieved alone and then destroyed her creation by greed and jealousy.

Janice Murray had been Sabild's secretary and book-keeper before she became Sid Murray's mistress. She had seen the surprisingly big contracts come Sabild's way and she had helped conceal the amounts of money that went as backhanders to secure them.

'Well, I'd worked in other places, I wasn't so green I didn't know what went on where contracts were concerned. But this was out of hand. Now I'm not pretending Sid Murray was lily-white in that way, but all this wasn't down to him. There was Billy Browning — he runs Sabild now, what's left of it — and there was *her* — Joan, that is. They were doing it. Chatting up the councillors and the council officers, mainly. Oh, you'd be amazed how much of their entertainment and what not I had to hide away in those books.'

So it went on, revealing Joan Murray and Billy Browning as the brains behind the business, Sid Murray as the small-time builder who found himself on a treadmill of bribery and contracts. He could not keep pace with the work and maintain a standard. Eventually there was an outcry about badly built houses and questions were asked.

Janice Murray said she believed it was the strain which killed Sid. He was sure the questions would not stop with those particular houses and the curious way in which their inadequacies had been connived at by council officers and planning committee members. And once one scandal had surfaced, the rest would follow.

Janice Murray was tender in her talk of Sid Murray, bitter about Joan, rueful about the way life had treated her. 'I have to admit, though, that he was very weak. Joan had always done what she liked with him. She'd wanted the money and the holidays and the big houses, but with her it didn't stop there. She had to have more and more, and she had to have everyone look up to her. Thought she was a bit of a lady, which was a joke.'

Rain said: 'I don't see why the Berrow Close house wasn't willed to you. I can understand that she might have contested the will, but I don't see why it was simply left to her.'

Janice Murray gave a thin smile. 'I told you, dear. She was strong, he was weak. There *was* a will leaving it to me. The solicitor told me himself, that Sid had made a will leaving it to me and then five months before he died he'd gone back and made another one leaving it to Joan.'

She sighed. 'Well, I've thought about that. Of course I have. I believe she knew the skids were under Sabild by then. That trouble with the houses, the papers and the law poking around. There weren't going to be many more big contracts, and Sid was too ill to do much more work by then.'

'But Billy Browning? He was still there?'

Janice Murray laughed, a happy rippling laugh. 'You'd see the joke if you knew Billy Browning. Now he puts up a good front, does Billy. Chatting up your councillors or what have you, fine. But ask him to sign on some labour to run up a few houses and watch him fall flat on his face. Can't handle the men. Word gets around. Can't get anyone to work for him. Do you follow me?'

Rain thought of Sabild as she had seen it for herself. Janice Murray was going on, smiling a happy sentimental smile. 'Now Sid, he was different. He didn't have the smooth chat and he mightn't always have been sure which fork was for which, but mention his name on a building site in Yorkshire today and the chances are you'll find someone who'll tell you he was a good lad and they're glad they knew him.'

'And after he died? You had to leave Berrow Close and . . .'

'Come here. Right. She sold it over my head. I was given two days to get out and the agents were measuring up before even that space of time had gone by.'

She paused, remembering. Then: 'I was told — it was all through her solicitor, of course — that I could buy it myself if I wished, that I was to be given first refusal. I didn't have a penny and she knew it. No, I don't own this place. I took myself into town and I went around the agents and I said who's got a house to rent? This wasn't a choice, either. It was all anybody had and I've been here ever since.'

She got up and Rain thought she had upset herself so much that she was going to evict them there and then. But Janice Murray recovered and said: 'I'm making myself thirsty with all this talking. I'll make some more tea.'

Robin was on his feet, too. 'I could do that, Mrs Murray.' He looked keen to help. Rain was amused. She'd tease him about this afterwards, tell him the second rule of interviewing: don't become too empathetic with the interviewee. Suspend your judgement; you might be listening to a pack of lies. The first rule was not to interrupt someone who was telling you something interesting.

Janice Murray gave him a flirtatious little smile. 'Well, now, it would be quite nice to have someone bring a cuppa to me. Off you go, then. You'll find everything on the worktop and you can see where the kitchen is.'

When he'd gone, she leaned over to Rain and whispered: 'He's a trainee, is he? He's very nice.'

Rain said he was coming along well. 'What's happened at Sabild since Sid Murray died?'

'Just what you'd expect. Billy Browning let the whole thing collapse. As I said, no one who's worth anything will work for him. And *she* — Joan, that is — is still milking everyone.'

'How can she . . . ?'

'Oh, I didn't explain, did I? She was never a director or anything official. She was clean, as they say, when it comes to the company being up to dirty tricks. I mean, supposing those council officers involved in the houses had been put through the mangle, they might have ended up admitting they'd done what they did as a favour to Sabild. And it would have been Sid Murray and Billy Browning who carried the can. Not Joan, because Joan was no part of the business.'

'So she wasn't legally liable. Everybody else could go to gaol for what she had done, but she was in the clear.'

'Exactly. So what does little Joannie do then, do you suppose? Well, little Joannie puts it to Sid and Billy and a few others that it could be very awkward for them if she told the police or the council — or the papers, even — what Sabild had been up to.'

'Blackmail.'

'After years of arranging for Sabild to bribe people it was only a short step for her to bribe Sabild and some of the councillors.'

'And that's how she got hold of Berrow Close.'

'That's how. It was always 'give me this or else'. I know what she's like. She did it to me, too. I didn't have any money, she knew that well enough. But I was to get the money out of Billy Browning for her, once he had tried to shake her off. She has squeezed Sabild dry but she won't see that.'

The kettle chose that moment to whistle. Then she went on: 'If Billy doesn't pay her what she asks when she asks, she threatens to report him to the police. Me, too. If I didn't persuade him, get the money from him and send it to her, then she'd tell the police how I helped Sabild conceal what was going on.'

Rain wondered how Joan Murray had been able to keep up the pressure, living at Nether Hampton. Before she could phrase a question that would not give away how much she already knew about Joan Murray, the answer came.

Janice Murray said: 'Billy has to send her cash, to be picked up at a post office. She has moved to Somerset and he has to send it there. Once, when he refused to pay up, she sent a young man to collect it. Billy had phoned her but he only got one of those answering machines so he told it what he would have told her. Then the man came. Billy says he was that frightened he ran all the way to the bank!'

Robin handed them fresh cups of tea. Rain asked: 'And this still goes on?'

'Not with me. I ignored her the last time. I thought, well, what the hell — go to the police, tell them what I did. Sid is dead, it can't hurt him and Billy was a fool and still is. He hasn't got much to lose now, anyhow. Do you know he even sold off Sabild's offices, one of their own developments, to pay off Joan Murray? Of course, he talks big, says he'd like to wring her neck and so on. But when it comes to the point he's too weak. She's the strong one. She always was.'

Before they left, Rain gave Janice Murray the Withy Cottage phone number, and Janice Murray gave Rain the address where Joan Murray had lived in York. Saying goodbye to them on her doorstep Janice Murray surrendered to tears.

'Phew!' said Robin, putting down the backrest of the car seat. 'I hope you got what you wanted.'

'She needed to talk. She'd never been able to tell anyone before.' Deftly she manoeuvred through the Saturday traffic. 'Just one more stop and then home.'

He sat up abruptly. 'I thought we'd finished.'

'We haven't found what we were looking for. *Our* Mrs Murray's home. Joannie's place.'

He groaned. 'All right, but if you go in, you go in alone. And I am not making the tea.'

'Yes,' she murmured negotiating a roundabout. 'I must talk to you about the tea.'

'What about it? I thought it was rather good. Strange kitchen and all that.'

'OK, OK, it was a great cup of tea. But you do not make cuppas for interviewees.'

'Why ever not? She was thirsty. You made her talk so much so was I.'

'Because you don't control an interview if you are kow-towing with cups of tea.'

'I don't think that was much of an interview. You sat there saying hm and oh and she rambled. Haven't you heard them on the telly, or the radio? Nobody gets to the end of an answer without them booting in another question.'

'They've got to work in seconds, and telly and radio interviews hardly ever tell you anything. Why do you think newspapers are still in business?'

'Gossip columns,' he said obligingly, and put the back-rest lower, signalling sleep.

'Don't get too comfortable.'

In reply he faked a snore.

The real Mrs Murray's former home was a brash neo-Georgian monstrosity in a suburb, all fibreglass porticoes and concrete donkeys bearing baskets of chrysanths. It was a tasteless piece of nonsense, neither old nor modern, neither one style nor another.

Rain said: 'Home, then. I've seen enough for one day.'

Robin opened a wary eye. 'Good.' He hoped she meant it.

The car skimmed across the country to the motorway. It was light and effortless and Rain enjoyed the drive, although for some of the way there was fairly heavy traffic and the run took longer than in the morning.

They came off the motorway and found food, then rejoined it and went smoothly on. By the time they reached Nether Hampton it would be very late.

Robin said: 'I wouldn't have missed today for anything. But no one would believe me if I told them what I'd seen.'

'You mean Janice Murray having a little weep over me before we left? And Bill and Ben holding us hostage? And Sabild crumbling before our eyes?'

'No, I mean that pork pie. Who would believe *that*?'

CHAPTER 15

Robin stayed the night at Withy Cottage. By the time the car rolled over the cobbles of Nether Hampton square it was too late to disturb Mrs Yeo at the Huntsman.

Rain dug out of the pine chest the sheets she had brought for Oliver. 'I shan't charge you Huntsman rates but you can make tea in the morning.'

'What, and lose control of the situation? No chance.' He flopped down on one of the single beds and yawned.

Rain said: 'Oh, you're not going to sleep again, you've dozed most of the way back! I want to talk.'

He caught her wrist and tugged her to sit down on the bed beside him. 'Come and talk then.'

'You promise not to fall asleep as you did when I was talking to you in the car?'

An arm slid around her waist. 'What do you want to talk about? The many Mrs Murrays?'

'I want to run through what we've learned today and try to get it into some sort of shape in my head. I've heard a lot of things, I've seen a lot of things. Now I want to think.'

'It's much easier to think lying down,' he said and moved over a bit.

She did not do her thinking until she woke a couple of hours later, cursing Adam Hollings for his single beds. Robin slept soundly, but she teetered uncomfortably and coldly on the brink. She might as well get up, get warm, get into the other bed.

She picked her way softly over discarded clothes, plucked her dressing gown from its hook and went downstairs. After switching on the electric fire and making a hot drink, she got the notebook from her shoulder bag and read what she had written at York, adding remembered points as she went.

She became engrossed in the pattern of events, not caring that sleep would not come and she would be drained later. From Adam's desk she took a clean sheet of paper and jotted down what information she would pass on to the *Post* for their news story about the murder.

This did not add much to what she had told them before, except that the dead woman had lived apart from her husband for several years before his death, that she had been left in his will a house in exclusive Berrow Close in York, and that she had sold it and retired to Somerset.

Until the police had told Mrs Murray's family what had happened, her identity could not be made public. Even then, of Sabild and Mrs Murray's connection with it she could say little. For one thing she had no proof how far Janice Murray's story was true. If it was proved beyond doubt, there were still the libel laws.

Holly Chase had told her newspapers investigated Sabild years ago but backed away from risking a libel action. Sidney Murray and Joan Murray could not be libelled now they were dead, but Billy Browning, Janice Murray and the councillors and council officers were alive and well and had lawyers.

Rain flipped the sheet of paper on to the desk and curled up on the sofa with her notebook. Then she sat thoughtfully for a long time.

Once she played through the tapes on the telephone answering machine. The spare tape had only Oliver's brief message for her. Then she listened to the other tape in which Joan Murray had pleaded with Adam. She curled up on the sofa once more, went carefully through her notebook again, and stared blankly across the room, concentrating.

Eventually she slept, to be woken by the thud of the Hampton House door as General Corning set off on his morning jog. Through a chink of curtain she watched him bobbing in a green tracksuit over the cobbles. His breath hung in the November day.

There was no sound from upstairs. Robin was apparently still asleep. Rain switched on the wall fire in the bathroom, slid into a hot bath. She sipped coffee as she lay there, her radio perched on the side of the bath.

Sunday. The local radio station brought her a cheery disc jockey who chatted to a vicar and then kept her amused with much banter and a few records while her bath water cooled.

There wouldn't be many more laughs this Sunday. She disliked Detective Chief Inspector Malcolm Merrett, but she was going to spend part of the day with him.

'I haven't any choice, have I?' she put it to Robin over breakfast.

He couldn't think of one. 'Are you suggesting you know who killed her?'

'I'm not guessing, but blackmail is a powerful motive. If only part of what Janice Murray says is true, there could have been several people ready and willing.'

'With Billy Browning heading the list, perhaps?' He took the last piece of toast, decorated it with marmalade.

'We've seen Sabild. We know how it's been milked, so Billy Browning must have wanted Joan Murray stopped. We don't know how much she made the people from the councils suffer. Maybe one of them was even more desperate.'

Merrett's car bumped over the cobbles to the police incident room at Laurel House shortly before nine o'clock. Rain went across a few minutes later, and discovered him in the hall talking to Sergeant Willett.

133

Willett's solid features eased into a smile of recognition. The chief inspector did not bother. He looked irritated by the interruption.

Rain said: 'Good morning.' Only Willett replied. She said to Merrett: 'I would like to talk to you. I've heard something which might be helpful.'

'Really?' He was mildly sarcastic. He turned his back on her and finished his conversation with Willett. He was in no hurry to do so. Then he pushed open the library door and strode in. 'Let's hear it,' he called over his shoulder.

He didn't wave her to a chair this time, but she sat down anyway. He chose to stand the other side of the leather-topped desk, studying the papers that lay waiting for him. His long fingers sifted them impatiently.

Rain went directly to the point. She had been told that Joan Murray was a blackmailer.

The papers stopped moving. Merrett looked sharply up. 'Who says so?'

She told him. His interest waned. 'That could be a malicious story made up by the mistress about the wife. Especially as the wife hung on to the money when the old boy died.'

Rain agreed. 'I don't know how much is true but I thought . . .'

'You ought to tell the police. Yes.' He thrust his hands into his pockets, the casual action of a young country gentleman in his library willing an unwelcome guest to be gone.

Rain looked up at the lean, fair figure, and held his gaze. She would say nothing, do nothing. The next move was his. *She* wasn't busy, *she* could wait all day.

At last he asked: 'Who was she blackmailing?' Rain told him that too. Then he sat down in the imitation-leather club chair and she told him the rest. A few minutes later she was striding back across the square, feeling foolish and angry.

'How was he?' Robin asked. He could tell from her face.

'Very 'so what?' He heard me out, most reluctantly, but he wasn't interested in any of it. An old woman gets murdered, I discover a possible reason and the policeman in charge of the case doesn't even make a note of what I have to say!' Her voice was high with exasperation.

Robin poured her coffee. 'Then forget it. You've done your bit. All you could do was tell him.'

She shrugged.

Robin walked up to the castle hoping there might be a police officer up there who could tell him when he could resume work. He had still heard nothing from Sir James Alcombe. Rain did some tidying and washing and went to buy the Sunday papers from the conservatory behind Jessie's cottage.

She was greeted by some of the friendly villagers coming away from it, and by a knot of them standing by the cottage gate. 'Jessie's that upset . . .' the beaky-faced Violet from the Huntsman was telling the old man with the interest in gossip columns and another man Rain did not know.

The papers were not laid out in their usual fashion for customers to help themselves and drop money in a plastic fridge box. Instead, loosely tied bundles were all over the floor and the plump jolly man whom Rain had met several times was wheezily selling them. He made a joke about the business being under new management, a joke that slid off the tongue in a way that suggested he had made it to every customer all morning.

He volunteered that Jessie was made ill by 'all them police asking her this and asking her that'. The doctor had given her a sedative, her husband was looking after her, and the plump man had done the neighbourly thing and taken over the papers. Rain spotted a lone *Observer*, and asked for it.

Beaky-faced Violet shot into the conservatory and said: ''Tis right enough, he's just gone in a police car, sitting between two of them in the back.'

The man straightened painfully with Rain's *Observer* in his hand. His jolly manner had quite gone. He shook his head in disbelief. 'Well, that can't be!' he said. 'Us knows it can't!'

By the time Nether Hampton church clock struck the next hour the whole village knew the police had arrested Wayne Chidgey for the murder of Mrs Murray.

In the Huntsman bar that lunchtime the story was pieced together. Mrs Murray had been attacked during the evening when she took Peppy for his walk over Laurel House lawn and along the Widow's Walk. She had managed to stagger back to the house but had collapsed and died some time later.

Initially, the police thought she had been attacked while most of the villagers were away at the carnival. That limited the number of potential suspects considerably. But once Dr Markell had ascertained there had been a considerable lapse between the attack and her death, the picture changed. She could have been killed by someone who went on to the carnival.

The Huntsman was an ideal source of information: Mrs Yeo was supplying meals for the police working at Laurel House, and, being Mrs Yeo, she had refused to deliver the meals, declaring that if they wanted their meals over there they could fetch them themselves, and what's more, they would have to order.

Covered plates were ferried by their colleagues for those who could not leave the house. Those who were able to snatch time made it to the quieter of the Huntsman's two bars and somehow, by the Nether Hampton magic, what passed through their minds while they solemnly chewed Mrs Yeo's cottage pie instantly became common knowledge. In this way it was revealed that any police theories that the death of Joan Murray and the still unidentified woman buried at the castle were other than macabre coincidence had been discounted. And even those villagers willing to believe Wayne Chidgey guilty of one murder found it impossible to blame him for two. His age, for once, was on his side.

Most of the village squeezed into the public bar that Sunday lunchtime to add their pennyworth to the tale, General Corning among them. He was full of nervous excitement and already an authority on the subject when Rain and Robin walked in.

'Naturally they'd thought about young Chidgey straightaway. Anyone would believe anything of that young villain. I know I would.' The General chuckled into his beer, pleased with his perception. 'So . . .' he drank deeply, keeping them waiting, pacing his story.

'So . . .' he said again, emerging with froth on his moustache. 'They haul the lad in and ask him where he was and who he was with. Well, he's a cheeky young blighter so he tells them he's got a good alibi. Says he was on a carnival float and if they don't believe him there are a hundred thousand witnesses, so there.'

'*We* saw him,' confirmed Rain.

'Mr Merrett didn't like that,' Frank Corning went on.

She said she could imagine.

'They had to let him go, nothing to hold him on,' said the General. 'But in the end they worked it out that Jessie's his aunt and the reason she was wandering about the village so late and finding Peppy, and then Joan's body, was that she was out looking for Wayne. The boys had put the float back in the barn after the carnival, but Wayne hadn't gone home and Jessie told his mother she'd walk up to the barn and find him.'

Rain said: 'So she didn't just go to Laurel House! That explains why I didn't see her torch. If she was going from her cottage to the barn she would have gone the back way, along the path. She wouldn't have come into the square at all.'

Frank Corning agreed. 'That's it. Jessie now admits that's what she did. Wayne wasn't at the barn and on her way back down the path she found Peppy and took him back to the house. The verandah door was open and in she went and . . .' He shuddered. 'If you ask me, she knew young Wayne had done it as soon as she knew Joan had been murdered. Covering up she was. Well, family . . . you would, wouldn't you?'

'But if Mrs Murray was attacked earlier in the evening, what does it matter what Jessie or Wayne were doing at midnight?' Robin couldn't follow the General's reasoning.

Frank Corning replied that he wasn't privy to everything the police knew, and he was just retailing the story as he heard it. He drank deep again. Rain and Robin exchanged shrugs.

'Anyway,' said the General, a fresh layer of froth on his moustache now, 'one of the other lads working on the float said that Wayne slipped off for a short time before the float set out for the carnival.'

'Where does Wayne say he was?' Robin asked.

'Home, only there was no one at home so that's not much of an alibi.'

Robin asked: 'If he did go home would he have had to go along the path behind Laurel House?'

Rain opened her mouth to say not necessarily. The General got in first with a commanding yes. For him, the matter was closed. Wayne Chidgey was guilty.

'You don't believe a word of it, do you?' Robin asked Rain as they sat on the pebble fringe of the bay at Stockway and watched the grey tide recede into the November afternoon.

She flung a pebble after the water. 'Let me be cautious and say I think my theory was a lot more interesting.'

'At least you now know why your theory wasn't entirely acceptable to Merrett. He had already got his man.'

'We haven't heard that Wayne has been charged, and many people who are charged are found innocent. Mr Merrett hasn't scored yet.' She flung another pebble. It missed and ricocheted back towards her.

'You will leave it, though, won't you?' Robin said anxiously. 'You aren't going to do any more snooping, are you?'

'Snooping? Oh, no,' she said, meaning yes.

She would not go back to Yorkshire again but she probably did not need to. She already had an idea that would test one aspect of Janice Murray's story. For this she would not have to leave Nether Hampton.

Now that the police had taken in a suspect for questioning at the town police station — the village version that Chidgey had actually been arrested was not confirmed — there was reduced activity at Laurel House. The indications were that the General's tale was correct and the police believed they had caught their man.

By evening, all the cars but one had driven away. Rain assumed at least one man would be left there until they and their papers were ready to leave altogether, perhaps when their local inquiries into the first murder were completed. What she had to do she would do whenever the house was unattended.

The police told Robin he could start work again at the castle the following day if he chose and that stirred him to complete some drawings and notes that had been ignored since he had unearthed the body in the ruins. Rain saw his light high under the thatch of the Huntsman as evening drew in.

Its reassurance that he was there was pleasing, and only partly because she needed his assistance to carry out an experiment concerning Joan Murray. Rain was also wondering whether to invite him to move into Withy Cottage and whether he would accept if she did.

Under other circumstances she would not have dithered, their time together had become precious to them both. Two factors held her back: Oliver and the Withy Cottage intruder. If Oliver decided to come to Nether Hampton it would not be easy to put him off and Robin's consequent retreat to Mrs Yeo and the Huntsman would be an embarrassment he should not be made to suffer. The intruder made Rain eager for company at the cottage but she did not want Robin, or anyone else, to imagine she was influenced by that.

She could put off her decision for a while, but the experiment must go ahead immediately. She found the pub's phone number in the telephone directory and asked Mrs Yeo for Robin. Puzzled at a call from Rain, he needed to be persuaded to do what she asked. 'Mrs Yeo will wonder why on earth I want to know.'

'No she won't. You can just wriggle it into the conversation.'

'Mrs Yeo and I don't have conversation, ever since I was unkind to that cat which always sleeps on the bar.'

'Then now is the time to make things up with her. Oh, go on, please Robin. *I* can't ask her.'

With total lack of confidence he said he would try.

'And ring me back,' Rain instructed.

An eternity later he rang to say he'd spent twenty minutes on uninspired chit-chat while Mrs Yeo wondered why he was getting under her feet.

'But you did ask her?'

'Sergeant Willett appeared through the back door and said he was on his own there tonight and could she manage one of her pies and chips. Being Mrs Yeo she said 'Yes, *but*'. The 'but' was that she was short-handed so he'd have to come and get it whether he was on his own or not. They fixed for eight.'

'Dinner at eight. Fine. Thanks, Robin.'

'Rain . . . Why do you want to know what time the law gets its pie and chips?'

But she had rung off.

Eight took a long time to arrive. Then she saw Willett come out of the gateway to Laurel House and walk the few yards to the Huntsman. She telephoned Laurel House, holding the answering-machine remote control at the ready.

It was only a chance. The machine Joan Murray had installed was identical to Adam Hollings's so there was a possibility that the control from his might activate hers.

But only if Mrs Murray's were still connected. Disappointed, Rain realized it couldn't be. She heard nothing but the sound of an unanswered telephone.

In that case, she decided, it would have to be switched on. She snatched a sheet of paper from Adam's desk, rolled it into his typewriter and quickly tapped out the names and addresses of Sabild and Janice Murray, and the address in Berrow Close that she had visited.

As she started she saw Willett walking carefully back to Laurel House with his supper. There were envelopes in a drawer of the desk and she helped herself to one. If she ever met Adam Hollings she would have a lot of petty thefts to explain.

But it was her growing suspicion that Adam Hollings was unlikely to return to Withy Cottage. Each day made her more certain of it.

Confidently, she went over the square to Laurel House, silently urging Willett to be eating his supper anywhere but in the library. No lights were visible at the front of the house, but if he had closed shutters he might have misled her.

Her footsteps over the courtyard gave her away. Willett came into the hall from the kitchen just as she tapped at the front door and opened it. Again, his smile of recognition. 'Thought I was all alone,' he said, swallowing a mouthful of food.

Rain waved the envelope. 'I just brought this over for Detective Chief Inspector Merrett to see tomorrow. It's not urgent, only what we talked about this morning. I'll put it on his desk, shall I?'

She was already at the study door, her hand going for the knob. 'Sure,' said Willett. 'Just having my supper, I was.'

'I'm sorry to disturb you. You carry on.' He didn't retreat to where a radio talked to itself in Mrs Murray's fancy kitchen, but neither did he advance any nearer the library.

Rain moved swiftly to the desk, dropped the envelope, pressed buttons on the answering machine and was rewarded by a tiny green light which told her 'Ready'. She swung another control as far left as it would go and was back in the hall and closing the library door.

The next step could have been left until much later when Willett might be relaxed to the point of drowsiness, but she decided to get it over soon. A delay risked him going into the library, perhaps to see what she had left for the chief inspector. Then he might notice that a machine which had been switched off was on again.

Besides, he wasn't a quick-moving man and she had slid the ring control to the point where the machine would answer after one ring. He wouldn't get to the telephone in time to answer before it did, and not knowing the machine was connected, would assume someone had been cut off.

141

Provided there wasn't an extension in the kitchen with him, her plan should work.

Rain dialled Laurel House again. And Joan Murray's voice answered her. With blackest comedy it announced that Mrs Murray was unavailable to take the call personally and requested a message once the tone had faded.

Rain sent the tape a signal from Adam's remote control. As the messages on Joan Murray's tape were repeated to her she recorded them on Adam's spare tape. There were twelve messages, from garages and dry cleaners, shops, individuals who gave their names and others who didn't. Twelve messages, and one of them was a threat to kill her.

CHAPTER 16

Robin's light went out under the thatch and shortly after he was at Withy Cottage demanding to know the significance of Willett's pie and chips. Rain played him the tape.

'How on earth did you get hold of that?'

'I recorded it over the phone. I'll explain in a minute. Listen to the next bit, and tell me if you recognize the voice.'

She saw that he did. 'Adam,' he said flatly.

'I thought it must be, from the context and the Australian accent. But I've never spoken to him, I couldn't be sure.'

'When were these calls made?'

'There's no way of telling. None of the callers timed their messages, but it's not like a business phone which is constantly busy with the tape being used up and rewound and used up all over again. This one could have taken months to accumulate twelve messages.'

The tape was continuing with its motley of callers. Rain said: 'And now listen to this one.'

A man announced himself as Billy Browning and went straight on the attack. Joan Murray was a greedy cow and he'd handed over all she was going to get. She needn't think he was scared of her. If she tried it once more he was going to kill her.

The tone, to begin with, was fierce determination. By the time it was threatening her life it was uncontrollable rage.

'According to Janice Murray it was after Billy Browning left the message that a young man was sent to collect the money,' Rain reminded Robin. She switched off the tape.

'You're thinking she sent Adam?'

'Aren't you?'

He considered. 'She *could* have done. We know from her taped messages to him that she was telling him to go somewhere, so it's possible she meant York.'

'And equally possible she didn't. Just supposing she *did* mean York. He could be there and back in a day, as we were. If he had had to wait for Billy Browning to get the money then it could have taken longer. But Billy Browning told Janice Murray he was so frightened he ran all the way to the bank.'

'So it was either a day trip or else Adam called on some of her other victims while he was in York.'

'Either way, a trip like that wouldn't cost much. Yet she had apparently planned to withhold some money until he returned. In her last call she gives in and says he can have it all in advance. No, I think what they were arguing about was a bigger, longer, more expensive journey than York and back.'

Robin suggested there had been two separate journeys for Mrs Murray, one to York and the later one from which he had not returned. 'He did wander off for a couple of days after I came to the village. I wonder whether he went to York then?'

'Do you remember when that was?'

'I can work it out easily enough from my diary. I'd had an appointment at Nether Hampton Hall to see Sir James Alcombe and I was looking forward to having Adam to grumble to over a pint. He didn't turn up, he'd gone away.'

'The other thing I'd like is a photograph of Adam.'

'Which one of us is going to be cheeky enough to ask Cynthia Brand for that?' Robin asked.

'Don't panic. I'm hoping to get one from his cousin. Oliver.'

She didn't burden Oliver with her scheme, just requested a photograph of Adam if he had one and promised to tell all as soon as they both had time to talk. That suited Oliver. He wasn't anxious for a long discussion and the telephone line was poor. He promised to look for a photograph, was sure he had one although it would be a few years old and she was to excuse the stuffed kangaroo in the background.

Monday was brighter and sunnier than it had been for days. Rain pulled on her warmest sweater and set out to walk to the Chidgey cottage in Mill Lane. The brown puppy met her again but this time Mrs Chidgey did not come from the back of the house. The rector with the Father Christmas looks let Rain in at the front door.

Mrs Chidgey was sitting, pale and tired, at the kitchen table, her broad face cupped in a roughened hand. Her eyes were red with sleeplessness and crying.

Rain's errand was to sympathize with the Chidgey's plight and assure Mrs Chidgey that she was not to bother herself about Withy Cottage. Mrs Chidgey did not look as though she had the strength to lift a duster, but was adamant she would turn up next day as promised. Eventually Rain had no choice but to accept that.

She tried to leave then but was equally unsuccessful there, and was persuaded to a cup of tea. Mrs Chidgey was making a huge effort but tears overflowed as she wielded the teapot.

'Our Wayne never done that . . . he couldn't have done that,' she wailed. Tea over-ran the cup and pooled across the table. The pot was set down at random and Mrs Chidgey sobbed loudly.

The rector, sitting across the table from her, patted her forearm, and offered soothing assurances that everything would be done to make sure that Wayne got justice. He was oddly formal.

Rain discreetly moved the teapot on to its stand and sought a cloth to mop up the pool. She was impressed that the Reverend Clifford Hadley was neatly avoiding sharing

145

Mrs Chidgey's conviction that her Wayne couldn't have murdered anyone.

As the greying dishcloth sucked up the last of the spilled tea, Mrs Chidgey suddenly clutched at Rain's wrist and lifted a tear-streaked face to her. 'Oh God, can't *you* tell them? He never done it. They would listen to *you*. You could put it in the papers . . .' The rest was unintelligible anguish.

The rector awkwardly relinquished Mrs Chidgey's arm. He eased his chair a fraction away from the table, and looked at the whitening knuckles of the strong coarse hand which gripped Rain so firmly.

Rain put her free hand on Mrs Chidgey's shoulder and said she knew not what. Mrs Chidgey was so loud in her grief she could hear nothing anyway.

The embarrassing tableau ended only when Violet burst into the cottage. Soon after, Rain and the rector walked back to the village together.

He said dolefully: 'What a tragedy for that family. They have been here generations and now something like this. Villages never forget, you know. Until the end of time the Chidgeys will be remembered for the murder.'

Rain challenged his easy acceptance. 'Do you think yourself Wayne Chidgey murdered Mrs Murray? That he is the type to kill someone?'

The rector shook his head, but it was no denial of Wayne's guilt. 'It is in all of us, the evil capacity for evil deeds. Who is to say why it suddenly seizes control of one human being and not another?'

'But you can't imagine yourself sneaking out and hitting an elderly woman over the head. I'd be prepared to swear *you* are not the type.'

He gave a rueful smile. 'At my age I'm more likely to be the victim than the assailant.'

'And even when you were younger you wore a dog collar and didn't have green hair and so the question would never have arisen.'

'The police haven't arrested him because of his outlandish appearance, you know.' They walked on in contemplative silence, watched by an inquisitive horse at a field gate, mumbled at by the roadside stream.

The rector had dutifully visited a parishioner in her time of trouble and, while he hardly expected her gratitude, she had brushed aside his words of comfort and appealed to a newspaper gossip columnist as a person more likely to be useful. Human frailty being what it is, he was hurt by the rejection.

Rain had been at first discomforted by the rector's unease at Mill Cottage, although one could hardly expect him to be confidently practised at dealing with such a situation. Her feeling had intensified when Mrs Chidgey had, literally, grabbed at her as a likelier hope.

Side by side they walked up Mill Lane, each thinking over their embarrassment. Then the rector switched to another theme: 'And that poor soul at the castle. Two horrors to hit a small community like ours in a space of days. Such dreadful coincidence. They don't yet know who she is, you know, but someone somewhere must be missing a loved one.'

The Reverend Clifford Hadley shook his white head again, at a loss to understand such evil in his quiet, friendly parish. He had relished writing about the village's bloody past, but this was different. This touched him.

At St Michael's they parted, the rector to go into the church, and Rain to walk up to the square and Withy Cottage. Detective Sergeant Paul Rich was watching out for her and met her as she was grappling with the stiff cottage door. He hoped she had time to talk.

His face was disappointment when he saw the dull ashes where there had been a vigorous blaze on his last visit, but he drew up a chair near the grate anyway. Rain switched on the electric fire and sank into the basket chair.

So she had been wrong about Chief Inspector Merrett. He had sent his sergeant to hear her story about Mrs Murray being a blackmailer.

The sergeant made copious notes and thanked her for her information. 'The force in Yorkshire has been making inquiries about Joan Murray because someone has to tell her next of kin that she is dead,' he said in that deliberate and painstaking way that had been so tiresome on his last visit. Rain asked whether no one in the village knew where her family might be.

'Sir James Alcombe had an idea she spoke about a niece in Yorkshire but I don't believe she has been traced yet,' he said.

He tapped his notebook with his ballpoint pen. 'I doubt if their inquiries would have thrown up anything of this, though.'

'Will they look into it now?'

'Bribery and corruption would be a matter for them. It'll be passed on and they'll decide how to handle it. Our concern is the murder.'

'I'd wondered whether there might not be a connection?'

He tapped the notebook again. 'A reasonable line of inquiry — if the old lady hadn't been done in by Wayne Chidgey.'

'Has he admitted it?' It was not so much a question as a criticism of his confident statement. He had once challenged her over her firm belief that Adam Hollings had gone away mysteriously, telling no one ('No one you've *asked*, that is'); now she would not let him get away with this.

'Not yet,' he said winking as he made the familiar policemen's joke. Then: 'So far as I know he is still denying it strenuously, but he wouldn't be where he is now if Chief Inspector Merrett didn't have enough to put him there.'

He paused, then added. 'He's a good policeman, gets results. Doesn't matter to him if he makes himself unpopular doing it.' There was no admiration in his voice, he was virtually apologizing for his superior's bad manners.

Then, as he drank a cup of coffee, Rain teased from him some more details of the investigation. She learned that according to Dr Markell's report, Joan Murray had been attacked from behind with a blow from a heavy instrument. This was assumed to be a piece of wood, because fragments of bark and traces of lichen were found embedded in her wig.

That immaculate bouffant wig with its thick curls had cushioned her from the first and hardest blow to the back of her head. Properly aimed, that blow could well have killed her outright. Instead, it had glanced and her killer had to strike twice more. A heavy bruise on her right forearm suggested she had raised it to defend herself. The angle of a second blow to her head showed it must have been struck by someone standing over her once she had fallen to the ground.

Fibres ripped from her peacock blue silk dress had been found clinging to a bush along Widow's Walk and her light-weight plastic torch had been recovered from undergrowth nearby. Both were evidence that the assault had taken place on the path.

Afterwards Mrs Murray had dragged herself along the path and up the sloping lawn, through the covered conservatory and into the sitting room. The trail of blood and mud made her route irrefutable.

Rain shuddered. Mrs Murray must have lived a long time with her fatal injury.

'Yes,' said Rich, 'Markell estimates the time of death at around 9 p.m. She put up a hell of a fight, to drag herself all that way home, and most of it uphill. A terrific effort, and then when she'd made it she haemorrhaged and died.'

It was now common knowledge that Wayne Chidgey had gone along Widow's Walk at six o'clock to join the other youths in the barn with the carnival float. Rich apparently saw no reason not to discuss this either.

He said that when they set off with the float, to begin its long journey to the town, they took it over a farm track and out through the farmyard on a lane beyond the village. Wayne Chidgey was the last one to join them in the barn, and during the hour that they were there he left them for a short time.

He told them he had forgotten the sash he was to wear as part of his Japanese warrior costume. The others saw him set off towards Widow's Walk on that errand and return from the same direction later. They could not be sure how long he had been away.

'This information, plus his reputation around the village, made us take an interest in Chidgey. Mr Merrett had him in and asked him a few questions,' said Rich with a satisfied smile. But he could not or would not offer any reason why Wayne Chidgey might have wanted to attack, let alone kill Mrs Murray.

The word in Nether Hampton was that nothing had been stolen from Mrs Murray and he confirmed this. 'Nothing was taken from the house, nothing from the body. Apparently she was in the habit of wearing quite a lot of jewellery, but it seems it is all accounted for.'

He shrugged. 'Perhaps he panicked and ran off instead of helping himself.'

Rain asked: 'Is there anything to show he went into Laurel House?'

'We haven't found any finger prints yet, although gloves would take care of that, of course. There's no doubt he was interested in the house. Well, you'd know that yourself, wouldn't you? Hanging around it late at night the Monday before she was killed, wasn't he?'

Rain raised a questioning eyebrow. He said: 'Sir James Alcombe and the General say Chidgey was prowling outside when you were all playing bridge with Mrs Murray. They say you discovered him.'

'I thought there was someone there. I never saw who.'

He grinned. 'Well, the General confirms what Sir James says and Sir James confirms what the General says. I shouldn't think you could be equally sure who it was, not having been here long.' He slipped his notebook into his pocket and stood up to leave.

'And Edwina Corning? She was there too. Is she so certain?'

'Mrs Corning is only certain she didn't see anyone.'

'Then make it two all. Neither did I.'

'I don't suppose it matters, Miss Morgan. Wayne Chidgey admits he was there on Monday night. He says he was being nosey on his way home from working on the float. He saw you all in there and wanted a closer look. So he says.'

She did not know what to say, although it was reassuring that she hadn't imagined the whole episode and frightened everyone unnecessarily.

Rich said: 'They were Mrs Murray's closest friends here, would you say — the Cornings and Sir James?'

'As far as I can tell.' She thought of Adam Hollings. 'And Adam Hollings.'

'The invisible man?'

'Yes. I understand he and Mrs Murray were very friendly.'

If the sergeant stretched out his left hand he could pick up the tapes of the disjointed conversation these two had held via their telephone answering machines. She did not mention them.

Rich took a step towards the door. Just one other point he might as well put to her and he would be away. He was buttoning up his coat as he remarked: 'Sir James Alcombe seems very upset by her death. Would you say he was an . . . er . . . special friend?'

'Yes, and probably the last person to see her alive, of course.'

He abandoned the coat buttons and looked up. 'Why do you say that, Miss Morgan?'

'He went to Laurel House the night she was murdered.' Rain remembered her earlier conversation with Sergeant Rich and her interview with Chief Inspector Merrett. Hastily she corrected that. 'I mean she invited him for a glass of sherry at seven o'clock. Then she invited me. I spoke to them at the meet that morning. He accepted, but I had to say no because I was going to the carnival.'

He left then and she watched from the window as he walked away over the cobbles. He paused near the Huntsman and added something to his meticulous notes. Then he was through the gates of Laurel House and out of sight.

Rain drove to Portlet and the *West Somerset Advertiser* office. Monday was a bad day to accost the editor as the paper published on Wednesday and work would be building to its

Tuesday peak. But she also had business that would not wait. She hoped they might do a deal.

The same young girl was toying with the same advertisement booking forms when Rain went into the front office. Jack Stevens bounced out at the message that Rain Morgan was there again.

'And now?' he said, eager to be of help.

'I'm offering a deal. A one-sided deal where you do all the work and I offer very little in return.'

He threw his arms wide. 'Ah, an honest journalist! I knew I would meet one eventually. What would you like me to do?'

Rain hesitated, looked around. 'First of all find somewhere less public to talk.'

He raised the counter flap and walked to the door. 'Dora's Café. She's as deaf as a post but the tea's OK.'

He led the way at his frantic pace to a corner café. A grey-haired bespectacled woman with a hearing-aid fetched them two cups of tea after a brief shouting match and some ambiguous gestures.

'Dora,' Jack Stevens explained superfluously. 'The deal, then?'

Rain sipped the scalding tea. 'I've been looking at the *West Somerset Advertiser* . . .'

'Ah, let *me* offer *you* a deal first. Don't tell me how wonderful it must be to edit a weekly paper in a beautiful place like this and I won't tell you what it's really like.'

'Fine. But you must promise not to tell me how you nearly went to Fleet Street and I'll promise not to tell you what the *Daily Grind* is really like.'

The pact was made. She said: 'I need some information from a local bank manager and I think you would have more success at getting it than I would. A paragraph in last week's paper tells me the man with the answers is the chairman of your Rotary Club.'

'Bill Tomson. Unless it's the combination of his safe I don't see why I shouldn't try for you.'

She told him it wasn't that, it was an inquiry about the state of Adam Hollings's account. Not how much money was in it, but whether it had been drawn on since 3 September, and whether any substantial or unexpected amounts had gone in since then.

Jack Stevens forgot about his tea. He whipped off his glasses and studied her intently. 'Why do you want to know that?'

She said Adam Hollings had disappeared and she was increasingly concerned that the circumstances were suspicious.

No promises, but he would try. And in return? She filled in the gaps in his knowledge of the Murray murder inquiry.

Next day he phoned with the answers. The only money which had gone into the Hollings account since 3 September was the quarterly payment from the publishers of *Publicans and Sinners*, Adam's aunt's novel. As usual the account was very low before that sum arrived. Nothing had been drawn out since 29 August.

During Jack Steven's call, Mrs Chidgey arrived, haggard and ill. She would not be persuaded to go home again and listlessly set about the dusting and vacuuming. Wayne had now been charged with the murder.

CHAPTER 17

Oliver had not found a photograph of Adam, with or without stuffed kangaroo in the background. Instead he had drawn a cartoon of his cousin and posted Rain that. It arrived on Wednesday.

'What am I supposed to do with this!' she demanded, thrusting it at Robin as they sat in the Yethercombe restaurant that evening.

He burst out laughing. 'Oliver's marvellous. Anyone would know Adam from that. Except Adam — I'm sure *he* thinks he's rather pretty.'

'I couldn't show this to Janice Murray or Billy Browning and say, "Was this the heavy Joan Murray sent to screw the money out of you?"'

Robin laughed again. 'They'd recognize him all right, if it *was* Adam who visited York, but he hardly looks much of a threat.'

'He looks like a malicious weed. No one would admit to being intimidated by this character.'

Robin handed the cartoon back to her. She said: 'Oliver was once told he drew people's weaknesses. He was rather pleased about that.'

The waitress came and they ordered. Then Robin said: 'So you were going to send the photograph to Janice Murray?'

'To see if it rang any bells. But I had another plan and that one has worked rather better. I've found out that Adam's bank account was at a standstill since a week before he disappeared.'

'However could you do that?'

'I knew where it was, of course, because of the unopened letter his bank sent him just after he had gone away. The envelope was overprinted with the name of the bank and the postmark told me Portlet.'

'Did he withdraw much money the week before he went away?'

'I don't have any figures, but I'm told the account was at its usual low level. That suggests he didn't. I think now that if Joan Murray was sending him off on an expensive trip then she sent him with a suitcase full of fivers.'

'He didn't have a suitcase. You told me, you found the neatest set of travel luggage ever.'

'So I did. Where is he, then?'

Robin groaned. 'Look, can't we dispense with Adam? With them all? I'll tell you what actually happened, then we can talk about something interesting. All we've talked about since I have known you is murder.'

'And blackmail.'

'And blackmail. Ready for the definitive version? Listening?'

She nodded.

He said: 'It was like this. Edwina Corning was running the local drugs racket. Adam was one of her pushers. Then he started in on the blackmail business with Joan Murray. Edwina was jealous and had him bumped off. Buried him, under that herbaceous border she's so proud of. The General squeals on her to Joan Murray. Edwina finds out and bumps off Joan Murray to protect her guilty secret. Wayne Chidgey is sleuthing about outside Laurel House and gets his fingers burned . . . What have I missed?'

'*Your* murder. I mean the woman you found. It looks rather suspicious if you don't include her.'

'Oh, she was just a junkie, a victim of Edwina's industry. Will that do? Now can we talk about something else?'

Rain leaned forward. 'They are waiting for an encore,' she whispered. There wasn't an eye in the room which wasn't watching him, not an ear which had not heard every word.

As he looked round the faces feigned deep interest in bread rolls and bowls of sugar. Jerkily the conversation at the other tables revived.

Robin and Rain disappointed them. For the rest of the meal they talked about Robin's next project. His Middle East trip was now only a fortnight away.

Sitting comfortably with a brandy afterwards, Rain found herself watching an overweight farmer's wife who had squeezed herself into a gingery brown silky dress for her special evening out. Her mind was instantly back at Laurel House with Joan Murray slumped on the floor. It was replaying for her Detective Sergeant Rich's story of events leading up to the murder.

For the rest of the evening the picture of the farmer's wife tarted up in her best dress kept interrupting her thoughts. It raised a question she wanted answered. For that, she would have to announce a coffee morning for the Cornings and Sir James Alcombe.

'I'm going to invite the Cornings and Sir James for coffee tomorrow morning,' she told Robin on the way home. 'It's a return match as far as the Cornings are concerned, and I want to talk to Sir James.'

'I thought the Cornings were more the afternoon-tea set.'

'Maybe, but I don't think I could keep pace with Frank Corning's appetite for cream sponge. They'll have coffee and biscuits and like it.'

Her car rumbled over the cobbles of the square. Rain took a torch from the door pocket, got out but walked up the pavement away from Withy Cottage.

'Where are you off to?'

'Something I want to check. Coming?'

He came. 'Couldn't you have checked it in daylight?'

'Yes, if I didn't mind being seen to be doing it.'

'Snooping again.'

'Just a bit. Look. What do you imagine that is?' The street light didn't penetrate beyond the end of the square where the width of the road shrank to that of a country lane. The row of buildings where Hampton House and Withy Cottage stood came to an end and a slender path led between the final one and a barn.

Across the road from the barn was a stone wall broken by a door. Rain was pointing at it. Robin said, with exaggerated surprise: 'A door?'

'A door to a garden. To Laurel House garden.'

'But Laurel House is right back there.' He made one of his vague gestures back down the square.

'Yes, and its gardens are a straggling couple of acres. I noticed that on the plan in the church porch. It's quite clear that the wall over there is a boundary of Laurel House.'

'But I don't see . . .'

'And if we go through this door . . .' She was across the road, her hand going for the latch.

Robin took her hand. 'We can't go blundering about in the grounds of Laurel House.'

'Let me just find out whether this is locked or not.' It wasn't. A stone path disappeared from the doorway into darkness beyond. 'And at the other side of the garden, roughly, there is the path that leads from Widow's Walk to the barn where the carnival float was. If someone . . .'

'Meaning Wayne Chidgey.'

'. . . wanted to get from the barn to Mill Lane and back in a hurry and he didn't mind nipping across a private garden, then he'd come this way.'

They both looked back at the path at the side of the final house in the terrace. 'And, yes, on the rector's maps this runs behind the houses.'

Robin asked whether there was a way from it to Mill Lane. They were already walking single file down the path and Rain did not reply until they emerged on rough ground beyond.

'There isn't one marked but there isn't a footpath marked directly across Laurel House gardens, either. He has marked the one that skirts inside the hedge below the lawn and makes a loop to Widow's Walk. Now, if you lived at Mill Cottage and had the choice of walking the length of the Widow's Walk, then through the churchyard and all the way up Mill Lane, or else slipping across this patch of open land, which would you do?'

She switched on her torch and picked out where the grass had been flattened as regular comings and goings had worn an unofficial path. 'Oh, yes. Look at that. It could hardly be clearer.'

Robin snatched at her arm. 'There's someone there.' He pointed along the backs of the cottages and she cut the torchlight.

A shadow moved in the shadows. They stood motionless but it did not recede or draw nearer. Someone was standing outside one of the shed doors which opened on to the track. They heard a gently persistent scraping as a latch was repeatedly raised and pressure applied to a door.

'That's Withy Cottage,' Robin whispered.

'That's my burglar.'

Rain ran forward and switched on the torch. The figure spun with a surprised yelp. A woman in a dark anorak, cords and headscarf. A canvas satchel was slung over her shoulder. Caroline Merridge, Cynthia Brand's horsy friend, was caught like a rabbit in headlights.

Rain said: 'I've locked it, Caroline. You'll have to use the front door this time like the rest of us.'

They marched her round to the square and into the cottage. 'And now,' Rain said, 'what is it all about?'

Caroline had recovered her composure, refused to look guilty. 'Adam Hollings,' she said. 'Had you heard . . .' She

158

glanced from Rain to Robin. '. . . that Cynthia Brand and Adam . . .'

'I told Rain,' Robin said.

'Cynthia was being damn silly, actually. I told her that but it took her months to see it. Then she broke it off. One would have thought that would be the end of that. But . . . I say, you haven't got a drink, have you?'

Rain gave Robin a hopeful look. 'Tea?' he asked ironically, a private joke that passed Caroline by. He went to the dresser and poured three whiskies.

'Thanks.' Caroline gulped at hers. She said: 'Actually, it was just the beginning. Adam told Hugo about his affair with Cynthia. Unbelievable, I know, but that's what he did. I thought Hugo would kill him. He was livid. In reality there was nothing he could do.'

Rain asked: 'Did Adam tell anyone else?'

Caroline took another gulp. 'No, I don't think so. A few people like myself and Robin knew but it doesn't seem to have become common knowledge.'

Robin said: 'You are not explaining why you broke in here.'

'I'm coming to that. That was because of something Adam had written. He mentioned to Cynthia during the summer that he had a great idea for a book. It was to be a new version of *Publicans and Sinners*. You know he virtually lives on the income from that?'

Rain admitted to having never read it. 'Neither had any of us,' Caroline said. 'One's heard of it, of course, and a hell of a lot of people must have read it in every language for Adam to have the income he does.'

'*I've* read it,' Robin said smugly. 'It's a soap opera about a small community somewhere in Australia.'

'Yes,' Caroline went on. 'I bought a paperback copy in the summer to find out what was so marvellous about it. As you say, Robin, the thing itself is just soap opera. But the jacket notes were all about the audaciousness of the author in using real people and a real place in her story. There was a storm when it was first published.'

Rain understood the rest. 'Adam's version was to be about Nether Hampton and the people around here.'

'Yes. We were all going to be in it. He said so.'

'Is that what you were looking for, a typescript?' Rain remembered the dishevelled desk when she arrived.

Caroline nodded and took another gulp. 'Adam told Cynthia it was ready to go to a publisher. She pleaded with him not to do it but he just laughed. He said he thought he'd made rather a good job of her character. A few days later she phoned him again, desperate. Adam said she was too late, he'd posted it to a publisher and he was going away for a while. When he came back he would probably have a good offer waiting for him.'

Rain said: 'Any chance he mentioned the name of the publisher?' She had contacts at most of the big London houses.

'Pegwoods. Cynthia remembered that because he told her he was sure they would be interested as they were outbid for the UK paperback rights on *Publicans and Sinners*.'

Robin asked whether Cynthia knew that Caroline had been to Withy Cottage.

'Yes. She was distraught about what would happen if the book was published. I said we could only see what damage he would cause if we could see what he had actually written. Then at least we would know how much she had to worry about. It was the uncertainty that was breaking her. We guessed he had kept a copy. The conversation just went from there and I decided I would get in here and search for it.'

'How,' Robin wondered, 'did you discover the back entrance?'

Caroline smiled. 'That was the easiest bit. Cynthia told me. Adam took her into the cottage that way one evening when he forgot his front door key. He said he kept the shed door unlocked as a safeguard against being locked out. The windows at the front are too small to climb through.'

'But you didn't find the typescript, and you came more than once to hunt for it.' Rain steered her back on track.

'The first time it was early evening, so I closed the shutters and went through the desk thinking that was the likeliest place. Nothing there. Then I realized that if there was a letter from Pegwoods it might give us some idea whether they were interested in the book.'

'So you took the two letters that were possibles and left the bank statement on the desk?'

'The two were postmarked London but they weren't relevant. I went to the bother of steaming them open but they were both junk mailshots, so I threw them away.'

Rain asked why she had left the desk in such a mess. 'No one would have known you'd been in if you had tidied up.'

'And remembered to open the shutters again. I know. But a car drew up outside and I thought, God, this is where I get caught. Adam's come home or he's let the place and his visitors have arrived.'

'You panicked. And fled.' Rain could imagine her fear.

'I thought I'd never have the nerve to do such a thing again. It's actually quite frightening.'

'So why did you? Especially once you knew I was staying here.'

'Cynthia and I were afraid you would find what I had missed. I had only had time to look in the sitting room. I didn't know what was upstairs and Cynthia mentioned a wall cupboard in the front bedroom. She said Adam called that his wall safe. It was where he hid his personal things when he let the cottage. I phoned to make sure you were out and then slipped in. The cupboard was locked and I couldn't force it.'

'And tonight?' Robin asked quietly.

'I brought this.' She drew a heavy screwdriver from the canvas bag. It was eighteen inches long and ended in a bulbous wooden handle. 'This was to be the final attempt.'

They all three looked at each other, facing the same question. Robin said: 'Honestly, I don't think we should.'

Caroline said: 'Yet if the typescript is in there . . .'

161

Rain said: 'We couldn't break into that cupboard without damaging it. If there is a copy of Adam's book in there then that is the best place for it. Tomorrow I'll find out whether he really sent anything to Pegwoods.' Robin's relief was audible.

Caroline left them, trudging off into the square where she had parked her van. She swung the screwdriver in her hand as she went.

Rain watched the headscarf bob away into the darkness. She shuddered. 'I'm glad I didn't disturb her inside the cottage. If she'd panicked again I could have got a nasty headache from that screwdriver.'

The headlights of Caroline's van swung across the cobbles and she was gone. Now that the mystery of the intruder was swept away, so was one of Rain's reasons for hesitating to suggest that Robin moved into the cottage.

CHAPTER 18

The Cornings accepted the invitation to morning coffee at Withy Cottage but Sir James Alcombe was waiting for the vet to attend one of his hunters and couldn't leave Nether Hampton Hall, even for that day's hunting. He asked Rain to drop in for tea that afternoon instead, if she would like to. She would.

General Corning and Edwina presented themselves on Rain's doorstep with military promptness and all would have gone perfectly if Laurie Pegwood had not chosen that moment to return Rain's phone call to the publishing house.

The Cornings sat themselves down and took an intense interest in the familiar furnishings — Frank stroking his bushy moustache, Edwina slimly elegant in a dark woollen suit, and both pretending they were able to avoid listening.

'Laurie, how are you? It's good of you to phone but I'm going to have to say I'll call you back . . .'

The line crackled that he was going out. She would have to speak now. Of course he would find out for her and let her know as soon as possible. She was grateful.

The Cornings still politely pretended they had not heard anything. Rain thought they were doing rather well. She relented.

'Rumour has it Adam Hollings has offered a publisher a novel set in this area.'

The General's eyebrows shot up. 'A novel? Is that what he writes? I've never heard of anything he's written.'

Edwina's features tightened. Rain watched, said to her: 'You knew he was writing it?'

'He joked about it — taunted, really. Everybody here was going to be in it. I doubt whether he wrote it. There was hardly time. One minute he was promising to write it, the next he was gone. I expect it was one of Adam's silly jokes, to see how easily he could frighten us.'

'You didn't tell me,' Frank Corning said, put out. 'First I've heard of it. Why didn't you say?'

'I saw no point in worrying you. The balance of probability was that he had not written it at all.' Her slender hand smoothed her skirt, a gesture to brush away difficulties. 'Or if he had, it wouldn't be good enough to be published.'

The General had coloured. 'You mean I was going to be in it?'

'Everyone, Frank. You included.'

'I see.' It was apparent he did. He sat crossly gazing at nothing at all, his moustache giving the occasional irritable twitch. At last he said: 'Damn cheek.'

Rain brought the talk easily to Joan Murray's murder. 'Jimmy Alcombe's taken it badly,' Frank Corning said.

Edwina remarked calmly that it had been a shock to all of them. It was not the sort of thing which happened to people one knew.

'Sir James must have been one of the last people to see her alive,' Rain ventured.

Frank Corning said: 'He saw her the same time you and I did, at the meet in the square. Never thought anything like that was about to happen . . .'

The gaze was switched to the plate bearing the biscuits. Edwina had sited it a fraction out of his reach. He shook his head sadly as the rector had done in Mill Lane.

'It horrifies me that Frank might have found her,' said Edwina. 'You know he jogs along those paths?'

Rain murmured that it would have been dreadful if he had jogged upon Mrs Murray.

'Went along Widow's Walk that evening,' said the General. 'They can't say whether I was there before or after she was attacked. Either way, I didn't see anybody.'

'And when did you last see her?' Rain asked Edwina.

'Late that afternoon, around 5.30. I went to the shop just as it was closing because I had run out of matches. When I came out I saw Joan at the gates of Laurel House. We waved to each other across the square.'

'Had she been out, do you think? Was she wearing a coat?'

'No, the purple tweed suit. She was very fond of that. She was going into the courtyard when I saw her.'

Again, the telephone rang inopportunely. Oliver, to say he had found a photograph of Adam after all and would she still like it. She gave him a York address to post it to.

Once the Cornings had said their thanks and gone home, Rain walked to the castle. She had space now to feel a shade guilty at being so brief with Oliver on the telephone, but not guilty at giving up missing him. He had stopped pretending he was eager to come to Nether Hampton, and she had stopped urging him to do so.

There was a light wind riffling the trees so Robin did not hear her coming. He was crouched over some earth-encrusted fragments that the castle had given up. She paused to watch his happy concentration, and remembered that other time she had watched him, when he had been asleep in her car. No one could see themselves concentrating, either, when the mind was so fervently engaged that nothing else existed beyond the point of interest.

He did not notice her until she squatted close beside him and said softly: 'If you'd like to move into Withy Cottage, you must promise to put the top back on the toothpaste.'

He flashed her a smile. 'Look at this. What do you suppose it is?' He cupped a curving, flattened object in his palm.

'Don't know. A bone?'

'It's a jug handle.'

'Is that good?'

'Not very, but I haven't found much so a medieval jug ranks high for the castle.'

'Not as high as a dead body, surely?'

He groaned. 'Rain, I'm trying not to think about that. Now look, that is where I uncovered the handle.' He indicated a point part-way along the trench. 'And I found these scattered all around that area.' He took up a handful of fragments and sifted them through his fingers. 'I've got some much bigger pieces of it back at the Huntsman.'

'Somebody broke a jug. When?'

He said that the mishap probably happened not later than the thirteenth century, because the jug appeared to be a green glazed type that had been made at a Bristol pottery. A century later the pottery had ceased to exist.

'A straightforward piece of detection, then.'

'Without any so-called witnesses making misleading statements, fiddling with the facts. The facts speak for themselves.'

Rain said: 'No they don't, you put words into their mouths. You are looking for a pattern, so when you find bits of green glazed pot the facts tell you the object came from Bristol. It must always be possible that in any particular instance the deduction is wrong. Supposing there had been a pottery here, making very similar pieces?'

'There is no record of a pottery at Nether Hampton. But I agree, there is no way of knowing for certain when one has all the facts. Isn't that where experience comes in? You make a judgement based on experience. *You* must do it, decide when you have got enough facts to justify writing a paragraph for your gossip column.'

'Journalists are a special case. We're worse. We'll get enough facts to make a story true, make it stand up. We'll run a story which says Lord So-and-so is having an affair with the chambermaid but we won't run one which goes on to say but Mrs Whatsit says this is rubbish. We know where to stop. We can kill any story by persisting with an inquiry until enough people put the opposite view so strongly that it falls down.'

Fat showery drops were carried on the wind. Robin did not look displeased. He slid the handle and the fragments into a plastic bag and suggested sheltering in the castle. They climbed over the broken circle of the wall and picked their way carefully to the gatehouse.

It was open to the sky. 'Oh, marvellous!' Rain said as the cold drops splashed down. He kissed her upturned face.

'Don't mock, this is quite good as castles go. There's more of this standing than of most others of the period.'

She pulled her jacket collar up, bundled blonde hair inside it. 'Why?'

'The locals have always left it alone. Most castles were quarried for stone but this place always had a doubtful reputation.'

'Ye mote that did runne with blood? And the unquiet soul haunting the Widow's Walk?'

'Just that. Perhaps the locals were more superstitious here than elsewhere, but they preferred to bring their stone a mile or two rather than risk building their homes and barns with the debris of a haunted castle.'

'And now two more violent deaths here and it's become a sinister place once more. The pattern repeated.'

Pigeons sheltering under a shrub that sprouted high on the gatehouse wall murmured rhythmically. Robin said: 'What's your new theory, then? That Wayne Chidgey is innocent, the castle did it?'

'Wayne Chidgey could have killed Joan Murray, although I don't see any reason why he should. I suspect the police have looked for and found a familiar pattern.'

'They have enough to charge him!'

'And it looks like an uncomplicated case of sweet old lady battered by young thug. Except that you and I know Joan Murray was not a sweet old lady and several people might have thought it worth their while to come all the way from Yorkshire to take their revenge. We also know that one threatened to do just that.'

'You still believe that's what happened?'

'She expected to meet someone the evening she died. Edwina Corning saw her around 5.30 wearing the purple tweed suit she had on when I spoke to her in the morning. When she was attacked she was wearing her peacock blue silk dress with the mink trimming. Sir James Alcombe seems to have cancelled his evening visit — so why was she all dressed up if no one was coming to see her?'

Robin thought it was unlikely she would have dressed up if she was expecting one of her Yorkshire victims. 'Besides, she could have changed into her dress before she heard Sir James had cried off.'

They were thoughtful for a moment. Robin went on: 'If she had been expecting him, or anyone else, there would have been signs of it. Food being prepared, a table laid. The usual signs. The police would have seen all that.'

'I don't think the usual signs existed in this case. Jessie always went in for the evening if guests were going to eat at Laurel House. When she was on her own Joan Murray ate what Jessie left for her earlier in the day or else she thawed something from the freezer. Sir James's invitation, and mine, was for a glass of sherry around seven o'clock. She did not suggest feeding us.'

'There you are, then. It was Sir James she dressed up for. He must have telephoned to say he couldn't come, and when she took Peppy for his walk she ran into . . .'

They looked at each other. Rain said: 'Who? Not Wayne Chidgey because I'm convinced he didn't go along Widow's Walk, but slipped across the garden of Laurel House and took a short cut to Mill Cottage.'

'So who else was around?'

'There were all the other lads at the carnival float — although they, presumably, have provided each other with excellent alibis. The General was jogging around the paths . . .'

'Rain, you can't honestly suspect Corning?'

'Only because I can't think of any reason why he should have done it. He tells me he jogged along Widow's Walk but did not see anybody, which presumably means nobody saw him, either. We know he has explosions of bad temper and he is certainly strong enough and fit enough to have done it. If we are just looking at the facts, as we know them, then he is as likely a candidate as Wayne Chidgey.'

'We know less about Wayne Chidgey. There could be things about his character which make him the obvious culprit.'

'If we were dealing with any night except carnival night then I would agree. But carnival night is different. Wayne Chidgey is a bored nuisance most of the time, hanging about the village looking peculiar and generally regarded as a potential thief and vandal. Nobody mentions that he has ever actually *done* anything bad.'

Robin was surprised that this was true. He conceded he had once described Chidgey to Rain as the local villain, but had not heard of one example of lawlessness to account for the boy's reputation.

Rain said: 'The most exciting thing in his life is the carnival float. He spends more time working on it than any of the other lads, it is his creation. All year he looks forward to carnival night when he is going to ride through the town with a hundred thousand people cheering him. So is it credible that on that very evening he should murder an old woman?'

The pigeons above them cooed complacently. The shower eased. Robin said: 'Wayne Chidgey is Innocent OK? Sprayed on every barn in the village?' The unasked question was why, apart from natural curiosity, she should be so concerned with the fate of Wayne Chidgey. She had not told him about that desperate appeal from the boy's mother.

'If I thought it would help,' she said. 'But first I'm going to take tea at Nether Hampton Hall.'

Sir James Alcombe was watching for her from the library window as she drove over the gravel drive to his disappointing Victorian mansion. He met her on the doorstep.

With misgivings she wondered what they would find to talk about. In the group at Laurel House she had noted his reserve, he was brought into conversation by others. They would, naturally, touch on Joan Murray's murder, but after that? She had no ready questions about his great interest, hunting.

His housekeeper, Mrs Wood, brought them a tea tray in the library. Rain recognized the elderly woman with her neat grey hair pinned in a bun on the nape of her neck. Mrs Wood showed no sign of recognizing Sir James's visitor.

Sir James told Rain in intricate detail the vet's opinion of his ailing hunter as they worked their way through Mrs Wood's scones and Rain poured tea from a fine old china pot.

Sir James's library was a real one, with the family's collection of books ranked along shelves. Many of the books were specially bound with the family crest blocked in gold on leather spines. As she was interested, Sir James lifted out some of the best of the books to show her. They were all about horses.

The library, he said, was his favourite room but he would show her the rest and she could see whether he wasn't right. He was. Some of the other rooms were clumsy in their ornamentation. No money had been spared by the architect but the hand that had carried out the design of the plaster moulding and the ironwork had not been delicate enough.

The library, where books were the chief ornament, was well lit by a tall window and the over-fanciful fireplaces of the drawing room and dining room gave way to a more austere pleasing shape. There was a round mahogany library table standing on a fine old kilim rug, and brass reading lamps. Rain thought irreverently that it was the sort of library where gentlemen used to shoot themselves.

One of the best features of the house was the iron-railed staircase that curled up from the hall, but Rain's tour included only the ground floor. The motif from the iron banisters was repeated in decorative ironwork in the conservatory and, she knew, it crowned the turret of the house too.

From the shelter of the conservatory Sir James pointed towards the Quantocks, picking out various combes and villages. Then, shifting direction, he indicated Nether Hampton church and the castle.

The Nether Hampton view was over a field, which was all that remained of the parkland of the former house. The village was largely obscured by trees. On the other sides of the house there were shrubberies, the original stable block and a kitchen garden. All in all, it was difficult to imagine Joan Murray as mistress of Nether Hampton Hall.

'And Laurel House,' Rain asked, 'that must be over there?' She gestured to the left of the trees which hid the castle.

'You won't see it from down here,' Sir James said. He led the way back to the library, along a broad passage where old prints and family portraits hung. Some of the faces echoed Sir James's, but their features were stronger.

He talked to Rain then about Joan Murray, hinting that he had grown fond of her, and repeating what a terrible shock her death had been. Rain was encouraged to believe that it was worse for him than for anyone.

'If either you or I had called in as she asked, then maybe it would never have happened,' he said.

It had not occurred to Rain to feel in the least responsible, but he had conveniently raised the very point that interested her. She worked around gently to her question: 'When did you find you couldn't go either?'

'I telephoned her during the afternoon. About 3.30. My hunter went lame and I had to bring him home. He was sick and I couldn't leave him so I rang Joan and made my apologies.'

He gave a wry smile. 'The police thought that was a bit strange, but they are not hunting men. Lose a good horse at this stage and the season's ruined. They couldn't see it. Well, they asked Mrs Wood and she confirmed what I had told them. She got a bit cross with the sergeant for doubting my word.'

The housekeeper came in to remove the tray. She looked shyly at Rain. Sir James told her what they were talking about. Mrs Wood broke into a smile and said teasingly: 'And it was lucky for you, Sir James, I remembered you telling me you phoned Mrs Murray and would not be going out before supper after all. It was half-past three, and a good thing I've such a sound memory.'

Sir James and Mrs Wood smiled at each other companionably and then she whisked up the tea tray to leave. He called to her as she was closing the door, but it closed anyway and Mrs Wood was gone.

Robin was at the cottage when Rain returned. He was not giving up his room at the Huntsman, merely intending to spend less time there. It was his answer to the question: 'What if Oliver comes?'

Robin had taken a phone message. 'Laurie Pegwood's secretary called to say no sign of any typescript from anyone called Adam Hollings. They also got their staff to check if there had been a novel of that type submitted under any other name. There hadn't.'

Rain flung herself down on the sofa beside him, kicked off her boots and curled up. 'This is turning into a very satisfactory day,' she said, and kissed him. 'Now let me tell you what happens next.'

CHAPTER 19

Murder was good business for the Huntsman. Police, journalists and the plain inquisitive made use of it. Joan Murray's niece had been traced and stayed there overnight before a day with police and solicitors and the train north.

The newspapers had been shortchanged. Until the next of kin had been informed and identified the body, the police did not release the victim's name. The journalists, of course, knew it well enough but until it was officially announced, the scant paragraphs they wrote could not mention it. And once Wayne Chidgey had been charged all they were allowed to publish was a report of his three-minute court appearance, during which the magistrates agreed to a police request that he should be held in custody.

After that the journalists disappeared like migratory birds. Whether they had ever reached the proportion of the 'swarm' Caroline Merridge had feared was very doubtful. The last of them, researching for a background piece to be published after the Chidgey trial was over, was driving out of the village as Rain and Robin walked down to St Michael's an hour after she had returned from tea at the Hall.

'God bless the Reverend Clifford Hadley,' Rain whispered as they studied the maps in the porch. 'Half of these paths aren't marked on modern maps.'

'It only proves they have never been registered, not that people have stopped using them.' Robin ran his finger along one of the rector's dotted lines. 'This one?'

'Looks right.'

They walked through the churchyard, took the track towards the castle and when another crossed it they swung left. 'This must be it, the castle straight ahead and Widow's Walk to the right.' Rain did not know why she was still whispering.

Underfoot it was damp from the morning's rain and the light was fading. The church clock struck six. 'Don't tell me — synchronize our watches with the church clock,' Robin whispered back, with mock solemnity.

The path looped around the castle ruin and came to a field stile where barbed wire attempted to keep walkers out. It had failed wretchedly and been torn down. They crossed it without difficulty and kept close to the hedge because all trace of the rector's path had been ploughed up.

Ahead of them lay the remnant of the parkland at Nether Hampton Hall. Going up the side of the field they came to a stile by a gate and crossed on to a track.

'This is where I first glimpsed the Hall, when I came for a walk at the beginning of my holiday. I couldn't see it earlier, although I knew I was skirting it, because of trees and the shrubberies around it.' She glanced at her watch. 'Come on.'

They walked silently, unobserved, down the tree-shaded path. Rain stopped when they drew parallel with a narrow wooden gate. 'We're here.' She held up her watch, peered at it in the weak light. 'Seven minutes, from when we heard the clock.'

The gate creaked open and they were in the shrubbery of Nether Hampton Hall, Rain leading, Robin hanging back unwillingly. Giant rhododendrons were excellent cover and she was confident they would not be seen. She walked softly forward, went out of his view briefly and then crept back, nodding.

'The stables are right there, just through the shrubbery. If Sir James Alcombe wanted to get to the castle, or the Widow's Walk, or Laurel House, he could be there in less than ten minutes.'

'Fair enough, but *why* should he want to?'

'I don't know. I'm just looking for a pattern. He's made me curious because he's lied. Joan Murray *was* expecting him, I'm certain of it. He didn't telephone her to cancel his visit.'

'But Mrs Wood confirmed it. You said so yourself, she told you as well as the police.' They walked slowly back the way they had come.

'Mrs Wood told me *he told her* that's what he'd done. What neither of them said is that Mrs Wood is very hard of hearing. That day in the village shop she wouldn't move up to the checkout because she couldn't hear everyone calling her. I wouldn't say her confirmation of Sir James's movements amounts to much.'

Robin said: 'Just supposing you are correct — just *supposing*. He could have lied to the housekeeper about his decision not to go out before supper. He could have told her he had telephoned and that he was going to the stable to be with the sick horse. Then he could have slipped out of the side gate and down the paths. What then? He couldn't have known when Peppy was going to demand to be taken for his walk, when Joan Murray was going to be on Widow's Walk.'

'I believe he could have known.' They were near the stile leading to the field. They leaned on it and looked across at the big house as Rain had done alone less than two weeks earlier.

She said, 'We were in the conservatory and he was pointing out the view. When I asked about Laurel House he said: "You won't see it from down here."'

There was a pause and then Robin said: 'Honestly, I don't think you should. Just for the sake of proving it's possible. You heard Caroline Merridge say how terrifying it was.'

'Ah, but Caroline was on her own. I'll have you.'

His horror was genuine.

175

The next morning Janice Murray phoned to say that Billy Browning confirmed the photograph was of the man who collected the money for Joan Murray. Then, in the afternoon, Rain and Robin went back to Nether Hampton Hall.

Robin had offered to talk to Sir James about the excavation. Sir James was pleased by the courtesy and suggested a tea-time call. Nothing had been said by either of them yet about Robin's macabre discovery when he had broken the agreement not to disturb land inside the castle wall.

'Why don't you gatecrash?' Robin suggested helpfully. 'It will give you half an excuse to be there. And you can come to my rescue if he makes a fuss about me going into his precious ruins.'

Rain shook her head. No, she preferred to let him have his tea and let her do what she had to do. 'All I ask is that by any hook or by any crook you keep him in the library for half an hour.'

'I'd better make that 'at least'.' Robin was anxious.

'Yes, please.'

She was wearing jeans and a sweater but instead of her leather boots she had soundless canvas shoes. She pulled on her fine leather gloves. 'Let's go.' It was a brave smile she gave him.

He drove out of the square and round the lanes, passing farms until they reached the road entrance to Nether Hampton Hall. He parked short of the entrance and let Rain out.

'Rain, you can change your mind,' he said. 'Come and have tea with him.'

'Dressed like this?' She held up a canvas foot.

'Or take the car and go back to the cottage. I'll walk back later.'

'No.' She closed the door. 'Five minutes,' she mouthed and trotted quickly away before he won the argument.

She could not be seen passing the main gate of the house, the curve of the drive prevented that. Not far beyond it she saw the footpath sign and climbed a stile. Soon she was through the wooden gate and in the shrubbery. She edged forward, screened by rhododendrons, and waited.

Five minutes after she left him she heard Robin drive over the gravel. Then Sir James was greeting him on the doorstep. So far it was going to plan.

The stable block hid her until she was ready for the dash to the house. Until then she was not frightened. Sketching it on paper at Withy Cottage it seemed so simple. The pencil lines had not made her pulse race in this dizzying way.

She argued with herself that nothing could happen. Even if she was caught the worst was that she would be made to feel irresponsible, foolish, impertinent. She wouldn't enjoy it but she would not be harmed by it.

Beneath her gloves, her palms felt damp. She rubbed them down her thighs, swallowed hard, practised breathing deeply and calmly. And raced across the grass to the conservatory.

She was crouched low beside it, working her way round to the door. It was unlocked. She was inside. Nervously she looked at her watch. She had wasted time dithering behind the stables. She must get on with it.

The double doors from the conservatory to the hall running through the house opened silently and she scuttled through. And then, half-way down the hall, where the passage to the kitchens led off, a figure appeared. Mrs Wood and her tea tray.

Rain folded herself into the shadow of a chest and held her breath. She and an Alcombe ancestor eyed each other with curiosity. The reflection in the portrait showed Mrs Wood hesitate on her journey, look around, and return to the kitchen.

What a time for her to forget anything! Rain and the ancestor contemplated each other impatiently until the reflection revealed the soft-footed Mrs Wood and her tray appearing again and moving directly to the library at the far end of the hall.

This was when Rain must make for the stairs. Robin would be keeping Mrs Wood in the library for as long as possible. He'd wanted to know how he was to engage her in merry banter if she was as deaf as Rain believed. Rain suggested her deafness was the best reason he could have for spinning a few pleasantries into a long and loud conversation.

She scampered down the passage and up the stairs with their fancy iron banisters. On the first-floor landing she stood and listened. A rumble of voices rose from the library. There was no hue and cry pursuing her.

She breathed deep and slow, tiptoed to the next flight of stairs and went noiselessly up. The house grew meaner as it climbed. The bedroom doors on the first floor were polished wood, the frames had carved moulding. On the second floor the woodwork was plainer and it was all white paint.

She had come to the end of the grand staircase now. The one to the next landing was uncarpeted wood, the banisters ordinary wooden ones. Stairs creaked. Rain went as lightly as she might, but made an exasperating amount of noise. Far below she heard a door close. Then, nothing.

When she had gained the attic floor she had a choice of three doors, each made of planked wood and opening on latches. Unlike the bedroom doors with their variety of brass furniture, there were no locks up here.

The first door opened into a long low room with a pitched roof and a knee-high window. Spare furniture and tea chests littered it and the dusty floor had not been cleaned for a long time.

She tried the next room. This was what she had hoped for. Here was the room that led up to the turret. It was empty except for a kitchen table and on that was a telescope case. This floor had not been cleaned either, but someone had been here recently: footprints were patterns in the dust.

Access to the roof was a door at the top of a short run of wooden stairs. Again she was fortunate: it opened at the turn of the handle.

Through curlicues of the protecting ironwork on the crenellated parapet, Rain had a magnificent view of the countryside for miles. She could look to the bay and to

Stockway and the Flatner pub on its rim. Or to villages in the Quantocks. Or to Cocker's Wood on the rise visible from the kitchen window at Withy Cottage.

She could see as far as the town. Closer, there was the jumble of colour-washed buildings that was the square at Nether Hampton. Closer still, St Michael's squat tower and the castle protruded from trees.

Laurel House was clear from this vantage point. The square white building with its slate roof, partially enclosed verandah and sloping lawn could not have been plainer.

As Rain watched, a light came on in Laurel House, in the sitting room. Detective Sergeant Paul Rich stepped out through the covered verandah and on to the lawn. If Rain had asked it, she could not have had a better demonstration.

Frantically she looked at her watch, realizing that this had taken much longer than she had allowed. She went back down into the room, closing the roof door soundlessly, then from the roof room down to the second floor landing. She tiptoed over the carpet to the stairs.

Coming upstairs, head bent, was Mrs Wood. Rain looked for escape. It was too far to retreat up the top flight. She had five doors to choose from on this landing and any one of them was likely to be the room the housekeeper was heading for.

Rain snatched at the nearest door, no time left to do anything else. A linen cupboard. *Please* don't let Mrs Wood be on her way for a clean tea towel!

Pitch black in there when the door closed. Fresh smell of clean sheets and towels, mingling with her unshakeable fear of dark places. Too dark to see her watch. Seconds, minutes going by. An age, or nothing at all. She couldn't stay here, she didn't know if it was safe to creep back out. Edging the door open. Glimpsing the empty corridor. Listening for sounds of the housekeeper moving in a room close by. Nothing.

She had to get out of the house. Robin would do his best but there was a limit. How long would it take them to eat a couple of scones, down a couple of cups of tea and discuss the results of a dig which had not found anything?

The answer was not long enough. Rain left the blackness of the linen cupboard, moved to the stairs again. Ironwork, red carpet coiled away below her to the hall. A door opened distantly. Men's voices rose to her.

She banked on it that if Robin was being given the tour of the house he would only get the ground floor, as she had. Keeping close to the wall she slipped down one curving flight to the first-floor landing.

Until she knew Sir James and Robin were back in the library she dared not risk going further. Even if she were to dash to the conservatory while they were in the drawing room, she would be trapped there, almost certain to be seen from one of the ground-floor windows if she went outside. She was only safe when they were in the library.

Supposing they did not go back there? She was weighing up the danger of trying to get out of the front door while they were in the drawing room or the conservatory, when the telephone rang. In the hall.

Sir James answered it, Mrs Wood perhaps never heard it. Rain saw him, his hand over the mouthpiece as he listened and simultaneously apologized to Robin for the interruption. She saw Robin, too, coolly relaxed as though he did not know what she was up to. It was an admirable performance.

Leaning back against the wall, out of sight of the stairs, she smothered a giggle. What a time to see the funny side of it! Nerves, she presumed.

Sir James was speaking to his vet, giving a detailed report on the state of his ailing hunter. Robin was sauntering along the hall looking at Alcombe ancestors, long-case clocks, the paraphernalia of centuries of rich living. Why, oh why, didn't the fool march back into the library and stage a sit-in until he had been shown every one of those boring books about horses?

She must stop watching them. If there was another scare she must know where to hide. The first door she tried was an austere bathroom. The next a dressing room. The next, presumably, Sir James's bedroom. Finally there were two bedrooms, both clean and tidy but with an air of being unused. The bedsteads were old-fashioned brass ones and she peeped beneath to make sure there was hiding space if needed.

Out on the landing again she was approaching the stairs, listening for clues from Sir James about what he might do next. She was so intent that Mrs Wood's sneeze on the landing above startled her to panic.

A silent race to the sanctuary of a spare bedroom. She turned the key in the brass lock, then lolled against the door and breathed deeply and slowly until her heart stopped thudding.

It leaped again. Movements in Sir James's room, next to where she hid. Mrs Wood? Sir James himself? If it were Mrs Wood, Rain could sneak past the door and escape. If it were Sir James he would hear her. The whole ridiculous scheme had been built on the fact that Mrs Wood was deaf and Robin would keep Sir James out of the way. No one had told her the telephone would ring.

Also, it had been a mistake to lock herself into this retreat. She could hear nothing of what was happening downstairs. If Sir James's voice floated up to her then obviously it was Mrs Wood opening drawers and moving around in his room.

There were a lot of 'if onlys'. Then another sound sent her scurrying to the window. Robin. Getting into his car, switching on the headlights and driving away.

Of *course* he had looked unworried when she'd peered down at him over the banisters. He thought she had finished and gone long ago. Now he had made his own escape as soon as he decently could and left her here. She unlocked the bedroom door, hesitated with her hand on the knob. As Robin had left, did that increase the chance that it was Sir James rummaging in his room next door? Or did it imply Sir James had just seen Robin out and therefore it must be Mrs Wood in there?

On balance she thought Sir James, however preoccupied he was with the condition of his horse, would be courteous enough to show Robin out. She slipped out of the room, passed the closed door of Sir James's bedroom. And stopped again. She had no plan, and no information to make one.

She went down the facing landing, the other side of the stairwell, and let herself into a bedroom. A frilly feminine room this time, not a room that had just grown out of a lot of hand-me-down family possessions but a room that had been deliberately put together for an effect.

Rain opened a wardrobe crammed with good-quality women's clothes. She shut the door. On the dressing table diamond rings hung on a ring tree. Rain did not touch anything. She gazed at the rings. They were not big and brash as Joan Murray's jewellery had been big and brash, this was fine jewellery.

She imagined they were presents from Sir James to his wife. When Eugenie had run off with her lover she had been careful about leaving behind what he had given her. And as he still hoped she would come back, he had not sold them although he was chronically short of cash. It was touchingly sentimental.

A cough on the landing. Rain peeped out and saw Mrs Wood going downstairs. She waited, listening hard. The library door was opened, there was a clatter of crockery. Mrs Wood was loading the tea tray. That wouldn't take long enough for Rain to dash to the conservatory. She must wait until Mrs Wood carried the tray to the kitchen and then pray she stayed there.

Through the iron banisters Rain saw Mrs Wood emerge with the tray and go off the main hall down the passage to the kitchen. The front door, then. Perhaps she could take flight that way. *Any* door, *anything*. She *must* be free of this house and its deepening shadows.

A third of the way downstairs she heard Sir James's footsteps approaching the hall and she had to flee to the landing. He dialled a number, waited, put the phone down and bounded upstairs. She flew back to Eugenie's room, held the wardrobe door ajar, ready to force herself in between the clothes.

Then she heard the sound of the cistern in the bathroom on the facing landing and knew she was safe. When she judged she'd allowed enough time she eased the door open and heard Sir James dialling in the hall.

The vet again. Sir James was checking something he'd been asked to do. He said he'd do it right away. Good. That meant he was going to the stable. He went out of the front door. Rain came down to the hall. Mrs Wood was making no kitchen sounds, Rain would have been happier if she could hear the clatter of washing up.

She went at speed down the hall and pulled open the door to the conservatory. A cat slid past her legs with a grateful purr and was into the hall. Rain had no doubt it would go straight to Mrs Wood and tell tales.

Well, let it. She was free now. Then she froze, her hand on the knob of the conservatory door. It was locked and there was no key.

Mrs Wood's voice drifted to her, affectionately admonishing the cat. No! Oh, no! Mrs Wood was bringing it back to the conservatory. Rain glanced wildly round the conservatory but potted palms weren't what they used to be. She could see no worthwhile cover here.

She sprang into the hall and threw herself at the nearest door. The ancestor with the reflective face showed her Mrs Wood emerging from the passage to the kitchen, just in time to miss her.

Rain was in the drawing room. High, wide and potentially handsome. More importantly there were couches that would hide her if anyone put a head inside the door. She sank down behind one and steadied her breathing.

The Chinese carpet and the loose cover on the couch shared the faintly musty scent of a room that is seldom used. Never again would she come across that smell without reliving momentarily her feelings during the minutes she lay, hiding, in Sir James Alcombe's drawing room.

Besides the fear of being caught, there was anger at her own foolishness. It had begun because of her conviction that

Wayne Chidgey had not been on Widow's Walk the evening Joan Murray died. Then she had considered all the other possibilities, Robin arguing against them.

It had been a mere brain-teasing game, but it came down to this. Unless Joan Murray had been the victim of that rarest of murders — the motiveless death at a chance meeting — someone must have known when she was on the path and gone there to kill her. If she had been attacked at Laurel House, or if Peppy went for his walk at a regular time, then the picture would be different.

Frank Corning could have hung around waiting for her, instead of jogging unseen along the paths, but if he were the culprit then he would hardly have volunteered that he had been in that direction at all. No, it was Sir James who interested her, because she felt sure he had lied about cancelling his visit. She had also been fairly sure that he was the one person in the village who could know when Joan Murray set out with the dawdling Peppy for Widow's Walk.

She had convinced herself that she must check on the view from the top of Nether Hampton Hall, and that it could be done cheekily but painlessly. Robin had persevered in trying to dissuade her, but he had not seen Mrs Chidgey's anguish, and, after all, it was Sir James who had helped point the finger at Wayne.

Now that she had checked, and proved she was right about Sir James's view of Laurel House, she would keep her promise to Robin and tell what she knew to the police. Then she would keep her other promise to him and stop meddling. As he kept reminding her, her argument in favour of Wayne Chidgey's innocence was that he could have no possible reason for murdering Joan Murray; and Sir James, who might have married the rich widow, had every reason to wish her alive and well.

Mrs Wood, sounding very close, was telling the cat how naughty it had been and she had no choice but to lock it in. There was the clunk of the door from the conservatory to the house being locked. If Rain had settled for the shadow of an aspidistra the conservatory would now be her cell.

Once it seemed reasonable to venture out again she investigated the drawing-room windows. Casement. No problem. Except that they looked across at the stable block, and there was Sir James popping in and out and doing whatever he did with his hunters.

The front door then. She reached it without hazard, heard the scrunch of the gravel and by the time it was followed by Sir James's footfall on the doorstep she was half-way up the first flight of stairs.

Crawling to the landing she crouched there recovering her breath. Sir James telephoned his vet once more, said what he had to say. The vet was coming out to see the horse.

Sir James ran upstairs, got half-way, changed his mind and went to the kitchen. Loudly he spoke to Mrs Wood. This was *it*. This really had to be *it*. Rain couldn't bear any more. If she got caught, then she got caught.

She didn't wait to hear what Sir James had to tell his housekeeper, she just assumed he would allow her time to get through the front door. She ran downstairs, giving priority to speed and not stealth. On the last three stairs she slipped, a noise Sir James could hardly miss. She regained her balance and snatched at the front door. There was his cry behind her as she ran into the dim light.

Adrenalin took her through the shrubbery, out of the gate, and along the lane. She didn't seriously imagine pursuit and Sir James might not have recognized her, but her feet didn't know that.

The path forked. She faced the first decision. Veer on to the one that ran along the bottom of the Laurel House lawn? Better still, do what Wayne Chidgey did and cut through the kitchen garden? It was the shortest way home, but the police were there. No, keep away from Laurel House.

Loop over the field and round the back of the castle, another shorter route? No, she'd be visible crossing the field and could be identified. Keep to the straight path on to Widow's Walk? She knew it best, she couldn't go wrong.

Gradually her pace slackened, but she ran steadily on. Trees darkened the path, cried in the wind. For the first time she was nervous of the place. Now she must be near the castle with the mote that did runne with blood. And now, right now, she was on Widow's Walk where the ghost of a medieval woman mourned her wretched end. And here, right here, Joan Murray had been struck down and left to die.

Rain stumbled over rough ground, slithered on damp leaves and came finally to the gateless gateway to the churchyard. She thanked her god, and moved swiftly between the gravestones. Two, three hundred yards and she would be home. Robin would be waiting for her. Soon it would all be in the past tense, a story to tell, soon it would be over.

And then she saw him. Sir James Alcombe's car was at the church gate. His tall figure stood inside the churchyard.

CHAPTER 20

Robin's brave joke that first day came back to her. 'All paths lead to the graveyard.' Now it didn't seem witty, it was mere fact.

When Sir James saw his intruder make for the shrubbery he could be sure to catch her. If she had run to the road he would have caught up with her in his car. If she had run the other way he had only to drive to the church gate and wait for her to come panting among the graves. Only Wayne Chidgey's secret, unofficial route could have saved her.

She dropped down, letting the jutting tip-tilted tomb-stones shield her. Options. Go back up Widow's Walk and on to the lawn of Laurel House. Think of something to tell the police and then get across the square to the cottage. Or go further back and take Wayne's route through the kitchen garden and hope to avoid the police. Or play hide and seek in the churchyard and slip out of the gate.

The last option appealed, because she could not face the shadows of Widow's Walk again. She moved from one grave-stone to another, catching glimpses of Sir James who was never far from the gate. He was unwilling to be lured away from it.

And then she was near the church, in the deepest shadow of buttressing. He was still guarding the gate but he had effectively cut her off from Widow's Walk, too.

He could not see her, she was sure of that. He sensed or heard vaguely where she must be, but he swung his head looking for a sign. She would give him one, the stone flung as far off as she could.

Gradually she slid down the wall, felt for a pebble, gravel, anything. Her hand met grass. Then her wrist touched something hard. She ran gloved fingers over it. A jam jar, waiting for flowers.

Clutching it, she straightened again. She could not attempt a very long throw after all. In the crook of the wall there was not enough room to draw her arm back far enough. She swung it gently and then released the glass jar with as much force as she could contrive.

It smashed a good way off, an explosive noise that startled Sir James. He turned away from her, moved towards the noise instinctively.

Now. Now she must thrust through the gate and run like hell into the square. Her step on the gravel, a gasp from Sir James and she was backing into the church porch instead. He had guarded the gate all along.

He had left her the church. That was all. He had stopped up all the other holes, driven her into this corner. And now he could wait, until he was ready to go in for the kill.

She felt her way along the pews, the wood icy through her leather gloves. The only cover was among the memorials that clustered in the chapel. There would be no other door to escape through, she knew that. She would not even try. Churches used only one door and she had come in that way.

So had Sir James. The meagre light from the west window revealed him standing at the end of the aisle. Waiting. Waiting for her to break cover.

She wished she knew whether he knew her identity. If he did not he might decide it was worth risking attracting attention by switching on the church lights. Part of her would welcome that. Part of her was already so terrified of this dark, damp place that light under any circumstances would only be relief.

She felt sick and faint as irrational, night-time fears gripped her. Yet she must be silent, she dare not become hysterical or defeated by them. There was a real danger to be faced, and that must be paramount. She must keep her mind busy and practical.

Now she couldn't see him. The church seemed so full of the sound of her racing heart, she doubted she would hear him closing in on her. Then she realized. He was sitting in a pew near the door. Calmly sitting and waiting.

Relax. You know where he is. He's not coming for you. Relax. And *think*. Don't think what *you* can do. He's calling the tune, think what he might do. With chilling certainty she knew.

The church clock had struck twice. She had been there hours. Rain leaned her cheek against the ice cold of monumental marble and resisted a yawn. The coldness of the stone floor had crept into her bones but she could permit herself only the tiniest movement. She had to be silent, she had to keep Sir James in view.

He was still in the pew by the door. Nothing had changed. What was going on inside his mind she could only guess. He would have weighed up his options as she had weighed them up for him. Forget the whole thing and go home. Switch on the light and see the prey. Or wait, just wait.

He was not a young man, he had not been eager to tangle with a prowler at Laurel House. And yet he had pursued Rain all the way from Nether Hampton Hall, trapped her first in the churchyard, then the church.

If he just wanted to know who his intruder was he could find out at the flick of a light switch. If he already knew it was Rain then he could tackle her about it any time, he did not need to intimidate her among gravestones on a November night.

Most strikingly, he was pursuing her relentlessly at a time when his hunter was lame and his vet waiting at the house. Horses were the most important thing in his life and yet he was disregarding a sick favourite to sit in this black church and wait for her to give herself away.

And when she did? When she sneezed as Mrs Wood had sneezed on the staircase, or when cold muscles cramped and she was forced to sudden movement, or when the dawn came and they faced each other across the carved pews . . . What then?

She knew what then. Once he had her, he would kill her. The longer he kept her waiting, terrified, the weaker her resistance would be. The inevitability of it surged through her.

She shifted her position, snapped her thoughts from negative to positive. She wasn't an old woman in a restricting silk dress. She was young and active and a match for him any day. She hoped it was so.

And if she was settled into thinking he would not move, then perhaps he was, too. Squatting, she inched her way to a different vantage point, near the Alcombe tombs. She still had him in view, whenever the west window shed sufficient light, but from here she could run across the nave if necessary or move up or down the chapel.

Velvet stroked her arm. Feeling up she identified it as a curtain. Floor-length curtains in a church meant draughty doors. She felt the bottom of a wooden door and pictured a vestry beyond. If she could get in there, lock the door behind her, put the light on . . .

Yet if she stood and the clouds parted, the west window might show him the pale patch of her face or blonde hair. She pulled the curtain over her shoulders and wriggled up behind it. The smell was dusty but comforting. Her right hand sought out a latch worked by turning an iron ring, the noisiest kind of door catch ever invented. She made her decision. The ring turned fractionally.

It took for ever — easing the ring round without it squeaking or grating, and all the time being unable to check whether Sir James was still seated or poised to strike.

When the ring would twist no more Rain pressed her body gently on the door. Bit by bit she increased the pressure. Finally she leaned with her full weight, flat against the patinated surface. The pulse in her temple throbbed hotly against the coolness of the wood, sweat trickled down her face.

The door was not going to give. Rationally, she had always known it wouldn't. And if it had, what help would it have been? A smaller trap. The vestry key would not be in the vestry. She could not have shut herself in and brought light to this horrible darkness.

The ring latch would have to be twisted back as patiently and noiselessly as it had been raised. Then she must try something else. She must force back the tide of panic. Panic destroyed reason. She must keep her head, keep control. She would not be killed because she was afraid of the dark.

But they were words in her mind, she could not act on them yet. For a while she stood motionless, slumped against the door, tears she would not shed burned her eyes. Now she did not have even the reassurance of knowing where Sir James was. He could have left the pew, moved forward to the monuments knowing, as she had known, that they were the only hiding place the church afforded her. He could be just the other side of the curtain. One movement from her and he could attack. Even now he could be considering the pink canvas shoes at the bottom of the curtain.

A blindfold was not a kindness to the condemned. It added suspense, it prevented them from looking on the executioner as he struck. The blindfold was a kindness to the executioner, not the victim.

She clenched the gloved fist of her free hand. She *would* get out of here somehow. There was no posse to ride over the hill and snatch her up, no hero with a long knife to cut her free of the railway line. Robin would be at Withy Cottage waiting for her. The rector, who lived closest, would be turning the pages of an old volume of county history he'd picked up at a church jumble sale. The police would be at Laurel House or negotiating at the Huntsman for pie and chips.

The Nether Hampton magic had let her down. When it mattered, no one knew or cared. She could look to no one for help. Incongruous. To be murdered in a country church and feel there was no one to look to for help.

She gulped down chill air, stood away from the unrelenting door and let the latch ring move slowly to its resting position. After that she turned round and edged to the side of the curtain. Peeping, she saw no sign of Sir James in the chapel but perhaps until she had moved away from the door it would not be possible for her to see the far pews.

Crawling, so that the monuments obscured her, she came out from the curtain and scrambled further up the chapel. If she wanted to be dramatic she would work her way to the organ and burst out full throttle with a hymn, something with an appropriate message. 'O Come All Ye Faithful'? Or she would clamber up the tower and ring the bells.

But she was not capable of playing an organ or ringing bells. And to do either would give her position away entirely. Before anyone had stirred from their television sets to wonder, she would be dead and Sir James would be home. So she would not be dramatic.

She struggled again to get into his mind. Surely he must be growing impatient? No. This was a man who would sit stock still on a horse in drizzle on a bitter hill until the fox was ready to run.

Surely he knew he couldn't get away with killing her? He would believe he could. Mrs Wood would not know he had left the Hall in pursuit of anyone. She would be prepared to swear he had been at the stables or wherever he told her. The vet, who had come to the stable and missed him, would be the weak link in his story but there was a fair chance the vet would never be asked.

Wayne Chidgey had been made the scapegoat for Joan Murray's murder. Someone else would be the scapegoat this time. Rain shivered, only partly with cold. High above, the clock struck the half-hour.

Wayne Chidgey. He had moved about the village innocent but unseen, guilty of nosiness in peering into Laurel House on the night of the bridge party. Sir James, who at the time had been more than doubtful anyone was there, had later told the police categorically it had been the green-haired youngster.

Rain remembered the strength of the grip Sir James exerted on the General during the struggle through the cloak-room window. He was an elderly man, in his sixties, but he was very strong and much taller than Rain.

Once more she came to the nub of it. If Sir James Alcombe had murdered Joan Murray there would have to be a very powerful motive, and Rain could not think of one. Surely he had no reason? Joan Murray was promising to be the golden goose and he was short of money. What was the point of killing her? Edwina Corning, the shrewdest of them all, believed Joan Murray was eager to marry Sir James. He was hardly one of her blackmail victims — he had no money and she wanted to be the next Lady Alcombe.

Car lights spun through the interior. Rain saw with a jolt that the rear pews were empty. He had moved and she had never noticed. Cautiously she looked about. Her eyes had grown used to the dark, the shapes and shadows were familiar and in face of the greater threat had lost their menace. But he had the advantage of her. He had always had it. He knew the layout of the church far better than she did, would spot the discrepancy of a shape where there ought not to be one far more readily than she might.

She put her hand against the granite surface of the tomb and inched up. Her face met the blind eyes of a medieval knight. Beyond him, stock still in the choir, was the slender figure of the lord of the manor.

Rain stayed exactly as she was. She needed to know whether he was facing towards her. If he were, then she must stay concealed, let him make the moves. He had become impatient after all. Maybe he had heard the faint noises of her movements with the door latch. Maybe he had heard nothing and begun to doubt she was in the church at all.

If he were not facing her then there was a slim chance of running across the end of the chapel and up the aisle to the door. She would have to be fast. He was alert and in a few strides could block the exit from the choir. Yet she must not wait too long. The only hope was while he was in the choir. Give him time to retrace his steps up the aisle and the trap had snapped shut on her again.

A distant whirring, far above, warned her that the clock was ready to strike the hour. He would have heard it too, known what was coming. This must be her opportunity. As the clock began to strike she would make her move, the sound of her initial movement masked by the clock.

It happened. She sprang to her feet, was through the monuments and racing down the aisle. As soon as she moved he was after her, breathing noisily but keeping close.

The swing door into the porch was only a few yards away. And then she crashed into something, fell headlong. It had caught her at hip level, something rigid stretched across the aisle from pew to pew. She collided with it at such force it clattered brokenly to the floor.

Sir James faltered when it went. Rain staggered to her feet not knowing where or whether she was hurt. Instinctively she snatched up the fractured piece that rolled on the polished wood by her left foot. It was a narrow pole. Her weapon was a narrow pole, a broken-off piece about four feet long.

Steadily she backed to the swing doors. Gasping after the exertion, he was coming after her. She held the pole with both hands in front of her. It wasn't much, but it was all.

She would have to get through the swing door with one movement. He must not have time to close on her, but to get through the door she would have to lower her guard. They both knew that.

Urgently she tried to remember which side the door was hinged. There would be no second chance if she got it wrong. The left, as she backed up to it. It ought to be the left, so that the door could fold neatly back against the wall. Otherwise it would obstruct the passage into the church because the swing door did not face down the aisle but came in on a right angle.

Correct. The left side gave behind her and she was backing into the porch. Just then Sir James lunged and she thrust at him with the pole, catching him, she guessed, in the chest. He staggered slightly, but enough for her to be in the porch and thrusting the swing door into his face before he could put his weight to it.

The church door stood ajar so she was immediately in the churchyard and breaking a world record on her way to the gate. Through the gate she went and up the road into the square. One look back to confirm she was alone and she covered the yards to Withy Cottage.

The light was on. Thank God Robin was there. There would be company and warmth and light. And food and a large whisky. And a bath, oh, yes, a hot bath. All that, in any order at all. She had never felt relief in such degree. This time it really was all in the past tense.

She wrenched at the badly sticking front door and flung herself into the living room. A complete stranger was sitting in her basket chair. He looked her up and down with cold amusement. 'Do shut the door, dear,' he said at last.

Her voice was weak. 'Who are you? What are you doing here?'

'I live here. I'm Adam Hollings.'

CHAPTER 21

Adam Hollings said: 'I know who you are. You're Rain Morgan.'

'So I am.' She stayed by the door, unable to think what to do.

He said: 'You are looking at me as though I were Lazarus back from the dead. And what have you been doing? You're filthy.'

Rain looked down at dirt-covered pink canvas shoes, smeared trousers, thick dust on a colourful sweater. Her leather gloves had ripped.

She said: 'Where's Robin?' Her voice had not recovered.

Adam nodded towards the Huntsman. 'He went to the pub — although it wasn't clear whether he was living here or there.' He raised a quizzical eyebrow.

Oliver's cartoon had been good, if unflattering. Rain should have known Adam from it: the carefully casual pose, his height and fairness, his style of dressing. But Oliver had given his cousin a hard, spiteful expression while Adam in the flesh was handsome. It was suddenly possible to see how Cynthia Brand had been attracted to this man of whom Rain had heard so little good.

She swallowed. There was so much she had to say to Adam Hollings, so much to ask him. She did not know where to begin. Or whether to. Or how much to tell him. She said: 'Where have you been?' *That* was the beginning, that was how *everything* had begun, wondering where Adam Hollings was.

'Aha.' A secret, teasing smile. 'Why does everybody always want to know where I go and what I'm up to? I'm not really all that interesting.' He sounded utterly insincere.

Rain could not remember why it was she had first wanted to know where he was. Oh, yes. So that she could check that it was all right for her to borrow his home. So long ago. Two weeks.

Parrying with Adam would have to wait, she had been through too much to indulge his guessing games. She opened the cottage door again. 'I'll be back, but I must find Robin first.'

As she stepped into the street, Adam gave in rather than lose her attention. 'France,' he called. 'I went to France. OK?'

'France?' she echoed. Ideas, bits of information were clicking together in her mind. She tried to sound casual but her voice was still not under control. 'For Joan Murray?'

He wore a sardonic smile. 'Joannie told you? Oh well . . .' An exaggerated shrug. 'I thought it was meant to be a secret.'

He'd come this far, she wanted to lead him the rest of the way, let him topple over the edge. A vague question, hoping for a definitive answer: 'Did you get what she wanted?'

He was flopped back in the basket chair, his long legs stretched out. He yawned. 'Do wish you'd shut the door and sit down, dear. You make the place untidy.'

She perched on the end of the sofa. And waited. Still hoping. He yawned again. 'Sorry,' he said, 'I've had a long drive back . . . What did you say?'

Rain assumed he was playing for time, spinning it out to tantalize. She repeated the question, as casually as she could. Let Adam guess it was important to her and they could be here a long time. 'I just wondered whether you'd got what she wanted.'

'Not what she *wanted*. I phoned her last week and told her I was sure she'd been fed a red herring. Er . . . is that what you do with red herrings, feed them to people?'

'You trail them about. To mislead.'

'Right. Well, Joannie had been misled. Or she'd stupidly got the wrong end of the stick. That *is* what you do with sticks, isn't it?'

Not explicit enough. Try again. 'What did she say when you told her that?'

He laughed. 'She said where the hell had I been and what the hell had I been doing. Words to that effect, you understand. *She* thought I should have been making progress reports to her every day.'

No help at all, yet. 'And how did you think you should proceed?'

'Well, I thought I should scout around a bit, satisfy myself I was not going to find Lady Alcombe and then wander off for a few weeks holiday before coming home. All on Joannie's cash, naturally.'

The right pieces had clicked together, the pattern had been formed. Rain said: 'What about the man Eugenie Alcombe ran off with? Did you find him?' She knew quite well what his answer would be.

He pursed his lips, shook his head. 'Nope. I looked for them quite seriously. Of course I did, it would have been a huge joke to have walked in on them. So I went to the village where the love nest is meant to be. Then, when that was no good, I went to the other villages around it. And then I took a squint at any ex-pats I heard of. Nobody had heard of them or anyone resembling them.'

'What were you to do if you had found them?'

'Report back, that was all. Knowing Joannie, she would have asked more but I wasn't going to make any pleas on her behalf, about a divorce or anything else, if that is what you are thinking.'

Rain hadn't thought that. She had been wondering how Joan Murray had planned to get money out of Eugenie, or

198

whether Adam himself had meant to try. He must have seen how easy it was when he went to York for her.

Rain asked: 'Did you tell anyone apart from Joan that they couldn't be found?'

He crossed his ankles, studied a carefully polished toe-cap, played for time. Then he said: 'No.' He did not look at her.

She heard herself saying crossly, 'Oh, come on, Adam, you know you did.'

He looked up, her tone surprising him as it had surprised her. 'Who do you think I told, then?' Challenging.

'Sir James Alcombe.'

Silence. Then the cold smile again. 'If you know all this why do you ask? I thought it was only fair to warn the old boy Lady Alcombe couldn't be found and Joannie was going to be after an explanation for his stories about French love nests.'

He laughed again, amused at his own wit, and told Rain exactly what he had said to Sir James. Rain was appalled.

She stood up. 'I'm going to the Huntsman now.' She cast around and found her shoulder bag where she had tucked it out of sight hours ago. She said: 'You won't be going out, will you?' If he were perhaps she ought to warn him about Sir James, but she was reluctant to be specific.

Adam came to the door with her. Across the square, light glowed in the library at Laurel House. Adam nodded towards it. 'I think I'll just stroll over and say hi to Joannie.'

'Joan Murray is dead. She was murdered a week ago.'

She watched him carefully. Amazement. A spluttering search for words. The real thing.

Rain said: 'I expect it would help if you could remember exactly when you phoned her.' She left him dumbfounded on the doorstep and ran to the log fires and subdued hubbub of the pub.

Her appearance cut off the rise and fall of chatter as abruptly as a plug pulled from a socket. They were nearly all there: the old man with the interest in gossip columns; the plump jolly man who'd taken over the papers; Jessie, looking

199

more anxious than ever; the beaky-faced Violet; Mrs Yeo in one of her strained frocks, heaving on a beer pump. The ginger cat, dozing on the bar, opened a lazy eye to find out why everything had come to a standstill.

Rain said hoarsely: 'Where's Robin?'

All together they told her, pointing the way he had gone. When Sergeant Willett came for his pie and chips, Robin had gone with him. Someone added that Robin had carried the cutlery, a gratuitous detail that would always stick in Rain's mind.

Through the iron gate she went, over the courtyard, into the hall of Laurel House. Detective Sergeant Paul Rich came from the library. 'She's here,' he called.

At the desk was Detective Chief Inspector Malcolm Merrett with his piles of papers. Standing by the bookshelves with their poor bric-à-brac was Robin Woodley. Rain went slowly into the room, her legs leaden. Merrett stood up with contrived courtesy. She dropped into a chair.

Robin asked whether she was all right. Merrett roared: 'Of course she's all right. She's just scared herself witless and wasted a couple of hours of police time.'

Instantly she was on her feet and shouting back at him. 'You've let a murderer roam this village, because you were so anxious for a quick arrest you picked up the first lad without a good alibi. Well, now you are going to have to let him go. I know who murdered Joan Murray, and I know why he did it.'

There was much more, but she was exhausted. From the corner of her eye she saw Detective Sergeant Rich move close to her. Robin tried to look as though he were not there at all. Across the desk, Rain and Merrett faced each other, neither of them flinching. Then the tension died. He cleared his throat, sat down and pulled the club chair closer to the desk.

Sergeant Rich said: 'I'll organize some tea, shall I sir?'

'Thank you, sergeant.' And Rich went out. Merrett took a piece of paper and scribbled. Robin asked again whether she was all right. She said she expected a few bruises but there was nothing a meal and a bath wouldn't cure.

'Very well,' said Merrett quietly, putting his pen down. His manner had softened. He was a personable youngish country gentleman in his library, settling for a chat with a friend. 'I'll tell you why we're all back here at this time on a November evening. We are here because of this.'

He picked up a batch of papers, sheets stapled in twos and threes. He riffled through them. 'The important ones are these.' He separated two and put them one side. 'This,' jabbing a long finger at one, 'is the pathologist's report on the body found buried at the castle. Dr Markell finds it was a woman aged around fifty. She has been dead at least seven years. The fractured hyoid bone in the throat suggests she was strangled, probably manually.'

He kept his clear blue eyes on Rain as he moved the paper to join the rest of the file. 'And this one,' jabbing the second, 'is the result of a search among dental records. She had very little work done and that was done abroad.'

He looked down, skimming the document as though he had forgotten what it said. He was timing, keeping her in suspense, as Adam had timed. Rain said: 'Eugenie Alcombe.'

If he was disappointed he did not show it. Without expression: 'Eugenie Alcombe.'

He dropped the dental report on top of the pile of papers. 'So what did we do once we got this report today? We came straight to Nether Hampton to have a few words with the lord of the manor. And where was he?' A wave of the hand dismissed the answers. They both knew them.

Tea came and Rain told them how Sir James had cornered her in the churchyard and then the church. Already the story felt unreal, fear was distanced. She ended with her return to Withy Cottage and meeting Adam Hollings. She repeated what Adam had to say about being sent to France by Joan Murray to trace Lady Alcombe whom she hoped could be persuaded to divorce Sir James.

Merrett broke into her flow to remark that she had already told him something of Mrs Murray's powers of persuasion. And then she told him how Adam had decided to tell Sir James that Joan Murray knew Lady Alcombe was not in France as he claimed. Adam had made one of his jokes: he had pretended that Joan Murray was 'convinced you've done away with her ladyship'.

After she had written a statement she and Robin left Laurel House together. 'I had to tell Merrett when you didn't come back, didn't I?' he asked apologetically. 'You should have seen his face. He'd sent his men off to interview a possible murderer and you and the possible murderer had disappeared together into the night. You gave him a very worrying few hours.'

'I haven't had such a great evening myself,' she said. 'Besides, if he'd got his man instead of harassing Wayne Chidgey . . .'

'Rain, Wayne Chidgey confessed to the murder! What on earth was Merrett supposed to do?'

'Confessed!'

'So Rich says. Wayne made a statement admitting attacking Joan Murray. Apparently he changed his mind the next day and retracted, but even so . . .'

'Why on earth should he have confessed?'

'Perhaps he thought they would stop asking questions and let him go home. People do odd things under pressure.'

She clutched his arm. 'I wouldn't mind being a fly on the wall when Merrett interviews Adam Hollings.' They laughed, the first time for a long time. Rain said: 'And I had to tell him about Adam, didn't I? After all, Joan Murray would probably be alive today if it hadn't been for Adam's silly joke.'

The food and the hot bath came at last. Awkwardly Rain and Adam shared Withy Cottage, Robin retreated to the Huntsman. He could leave Nether Hampton at any time, in a couple of weeks he would be working in the Middle East. Rain planned to get out of the village as soon as the police said she was free to go. All of it was all over.

She wanted this day out of her head. The fear and indignity were best forgotten quickly. She was not culpable as Adam Hollings was culpable but she had meddled dangerously.

She slept late, a long sleep unhindered by the nightmares she had earned. Adam Hollings woke her to take a telephone call. Oliver. She dragged on her dressing gown and went downstairs. Oliver was chirpy. Was she still having a wonderful time? So old Adam had turned up, all in one piece? How was she getting along with him? Good news: her friend who was losing his job on the *Daily Post* had accepted a better one on a rival paper. More good news: Oliver had arranged a long weekend off and would be setting off that evening to join her.

She raised difficulties, tried to put him off. Oliver rattled on, barely listening to her. Adam watched with his cold little smile. She knew enough by now to gauge what he was thinking. Afterwards she said: 'I wouldn't, Adam. The police could so easily find out you helped Joan Murray blackmail Billy Browning in York.'

His jaw dropped. While he was at a loss she tossed him a question a lot of people would like answered. 'Your novel about Nether Hampton — it was just one of your jokes, wasn't it?' He nodded guiltily, like a little boy caught at something naughty.

She shut herself in the bathroom where she soaked for a long time and examined angry patches where bruises were forming. When she reappeared in the living room Detective Sergeant Paul Rich was there, asking Adam to go to Laurel House to be interviewed by Detective Chief Inspector Merrett. Adam gave Rain a wary look and went meekly.

'The mystery man,' said the sergeant, staring after him. He spotted a new travel bag beside the desk. 'Him moving in or you moving out?'

'That must be Adam's.' So that was it, he'd bought a fashionable new bag for the French trip. Why not? The collection she had found covered every other style which had been popular in recent years.

She added: 'I want to move out, though. How long will you need me here?' He said they wouldn't but would like to know where she would be.

'Then I'll go today.' She would settle up what was owed to Adam in cash and in kind and she would go.

'You'll get somewhere else in the village, will you?'

'No, I'm going right away. Probably home.'

Sergeant Rich nodded, understanding. He said: 'We had Mr Hadley, the rector, in to see us first thing this morning. Seems a vandal has snapped the pole of his Friendly Society board. He says it's a considerable treasure. Must have given it a hell of a crack.' He grinned, knowingly.

'You didn't tell him it was me?'

'Not much we would want people to know at this stage.'

She pumped him about what stage had been reached. He said: 'Sir James is making statements about both murders. He reckons his wife was killed by accident when they were having a row about her carrying on with other men. He put the body down the well at the castle thinking it wouldn't be found until after his time.'

'He's an old man, he was nearly right. That would explain why he wouldn't sell the ruin or let anyone excavate it thoroughly. And Joan Murray was killed because he thought she guessed he had killed his wife. I couldn't work out what possible reason he had to kill Mrs Murray.'

Sergeant Rich smiled a satisfied smile. 'I've never arrested a lord of the manor before.'

'But what happens to Wayne Chidgey now?'

'No one's thrown away the key.'

Sergeant Rich looked with disappointment at the empty grate beside him. He always remembered Withy Cottage for its welcoming log fire on the day of the downpour. He said: 'You could say there was no reason for Joan Murray to be killed. Dental records name victims, not murderers. If he'd kept his head he might have got away with it. Instead he killed Joan Murray in panic, because of what he believed she knew.'

They were silent. Rain shivered, although the electric fire kept the room cosy. Her voice was a whisper when she said: 'He thought I knew, too, didn't he?'

'Yes, I rather think he did.'

'And Adam? What was he going to do about Adam? Kill him, too?'

'Mr Hollings wasn't here, was he? And unless he let Sir James think *he* believed Sir James had murdered his wife, then he wasn't in danger.'

The door of Hampton House thudded as one of the Cornings went out. Sergeant Rich nodded in the direction of the sound. 'The General had been saying his wife had seen letters from France to Sir James, letters from Lady Alcombe. But when we asked her she said she'd once been shown an envelope posted from France but hadn't read any letter.'

'I heard him asking in the post office for a stamp to write to France.'

'He worked quite hard on giving the impression his wife was there.'

Rain said: 'It wasn't flawless. Frank Corning couldn't understand the strategy that let Eugenie *and* the money escape, or Eugenie's bad manners in snubbing Edwina.' Another thought. 'And the General was quite puzzled that there had been a secret lover who had never featured in any of Eugenie's rumours.'

'Yes, the General seems to have had a soft spot for Eugenie Alcombe.' He gave his knowing grin again.

Rain telephoned Holly Chase at her home as soon as she was alone again. 'Holly, do anything, even elope with him if you have to, but don't let Oliver come here.'

Holly shrieked with laughter. 'Hey, I'm the girl who was told to post him to you first class. So what happened?'

'You wouldn't understand,' Rain said primly.

Holly shrieked again. 'Bet I would, too. What's he like?'

Holly promised to deflect Oliver from Nether Hampton. Rain packed her belongings into her car. Robin saw her from his room under the Huntsman's thatch and came over.

'You're going?' Inevitably. It was all over.

'Once Adam's finished with the police and I've settled up with him.'

'What are the police going to do about you breaking into Nether Hampton Hall?'

'Not a thing. The door was open. I trespassed and that's not a crime. Not, I think, that I would care to do it again.'

They walked down through the square, not going anywhere particular, just being together. They passed the village shop busy with Saturday trade; the cottage where Jessie's husband was selling newspapers in his conservatory again; passed the rectory where the Father Christmassy rector was upset about his Friendly Society board; through the church gate.

'Tranquil enough, now,' Rain whispered as they slipped into St Michael's. There was a pale shape on the wall where the Friendly Society board had hung. The pieces had been taken away. Facing it across the aisle the memorial plaque to Sir James's father. A name, two dates, a motto: 'Steadfast'.

Daylight transformed everything. The chapel with the monuments was a Sunday School corner, where children's innocent paintings were displayed. The velvet curtain was blue and did indeed lead to the vestry. Rain turned the ring latch. It was extremely noisy.

Neither of them spoke. Rain ran a hand over the wide-eyed granite knight, wondered at her luck in moving stealthily in this space which she now saw was littered with hazards: a brass flower jug, some children's chairs, a neat stack of hymn books. She might have toppled any of them.

Here, where the generations of Nether Hampton met, she had confronted her childhood fear, and it had been dispelled. Mere darkness and imaginings could not hold her in terror ever again, because she had been beyond that, to reality.

'I'm glad I've seen it like this,' she said as they emerged. 'I'd rather remember it in daylight.'

'You were frightened coming in,' he said.

'Was I?'

'Lip-bitingly tense. All the things you are usually not.'

'I've just had a lot of practice.'

The sky darkened, a shower swept over the square, pitting clothes, stinging skin. Adam Hollings wasn't home. They went into Withy Cottage to wait for him. Rain made a pot of coffee. They didn't talk much.

Robin sat on the sofa and looked through a newspaper Adam had bought. Rain rounded up coffee cups, sugar, milk. She called through from the kitchen: 'What were they for? Those observation towers on houses like Nether Hampton Hall?'

'For ladies to take the air privately. They're called widow's walks.'

She did not answer. The coffee pot completed its gurgling and she lifted it to pour. Through the window, beyond the cottage garden and its row of sheds, the hill rose grey in drizzle. The hunt moved across it, a blur of hounds, riders, horses. She could not see the fox but her heart was with it.

THE END

THE JOFFE BOOKS STORY

We began in 2014 when Jasper agreed to publish his mum's much-rejected romance novel and it became a bestseller.

Since then we've grown into the largest independent publisher in the UK. We're extremely proud to publish some of the very best writers in the world, including Joy Ellis, Faith Martin, Caro Ramsay, Helen Forrester, Simon Brett and Robert Goddard. Everyone at Joffe Books loves reading and we never forget that it all begins with the magic of an author telling a story.

We are proud to publish talented first-time authors, as well as established writers whose books we love introducing to a new generation of readers.

We have been shortlisted for Independent Publisher of the Year at the British Book Awards three times, in 2020, 2021 and 2022, and for the Diversity and Inclusivity Award at the Independent Publishing Awards in 2022.

We built this company with your help, and we love to hear from you, so please email us about absolutely anything bookish at feedback@joffebooks.com

If you want to receive free books every Friday and hear about all our new releases, join our mailing list: www.joffebooks.com/contact

And when you tell your friends about us, just remember: it's pronounced Joffe as in coffee or toffee!

Made in the USA
Coppell, TX
30 July 2024

35372623R00125